THE SH

Alison Prince was born in Beckenham, Kent, of a Scottish mother and Yorkshire father. She won a scholarship to the Slade School of Fine Art and began a teaching career on leaving college, but soon moved into freelance writing and illustration. For eight years she ran a small farm in Suffolk, then moved to a village near Stamford, in Lincolnshire. She now lives in Scotland, on the Isle of Arran. She has three grown-up children.

ALISON PRINCE

The Sherwood Hero

MACMILLAN

CHILDREN'S BOOKS

First published 1995 by Macmillan Children's Books
a division of Macmillan Publishers Ltd
25 Eccleston Place, London SW1W 9NF
and Basingstoke

Associated companies throughout the world

ISBN 0 330 33724 6

1 3 5 7 9 8 6 4 2

A CIP catalogue record for this book is available from
the British Library

Phototypeset by Intype, London
Printed by Mackays of Chatham PLC, Kent

For my daughter, Samantha

CHAPTER 1

Willa Pargett was weird. It was a bit of a let-down, Angie and I thought, after Miss Currie had gone on so much about this famous author who was going to visit the school. We'd expected someone really glamorous, or at the very least, dead smart, with high heels and a briefcase and a television smile. I mean, they'd sent Murdo Guthrie down to Mr Harris in Woodwork, just to be on the safe side, and the chairs in the library were set out in a half-circle, not round the tables like they usually were. Someone had even put a glass of water on the table, in case the famous author got a frog in her throat.

Then Mr McInch brought this woman in. If my mum had been there, she'd have said, 'What *does* she look like?' Willa Pargett was nearly as old as my gran who died last year, but much untidier. She wore black Reebok boots and striped cotton trousers, with a denim shirt that had its sleeves rolled up, and some kind of embroid-ered waistcoat. With fringes. And her hair was mouse-to-white, shortish, but really manky, as if she just hacked a bit off it when she couldn't see out any more. We were all completely gobsmacked.

Somebody made one of those swallowing noises that sound as if you've been thumped between the shoulderblades, and there was a bit of giggling. Mr McInch glared at us and said we were delighted to welcome Willa Pargett, to give us some insights which would help us with our Novel-Writing Project. We all clapped. I heard Ross Craig say, 'Willie Pargett!' and there was more giggling, because everyone giggled about willies. Mr McInch stood up again and gave us the bit about expecting everyone to be on their best behaviour for our guest, so we knew there'd be detention if we didn't shut up. The writer was fishing in her African basket for her glasses, which turned out to be the little half-moon sort.

She looked over the top of them at the window and the view of the science block, and said, 'This school's absolutely horrible, isn't it. No trees. I'd go mad if I was here all the time.'

Jimmy Kelso muttered, 'Mad already,' but we were mostly too polite to say anything – or too flattened by Mr McInch's glare. You could tell the writer was trying hard to be on our level, she smiled a lot and tried to use short words, but it was no good really, not when she sounded so ladylike. Then she said, 'Do you ever imagine you were somewhere else?' And she paused, hoping for an answer.

Nobody said anything. We didn't know if we were supposed to, and anyway, fancy asking something like that. It's private. I thought for a moment of the forest, but I wasn't going to mention that, not in front of everyone else. Then Ross said, 'Aye, Rangers on a Sa'urday,' and there was a bit of a cheer. Mr McInch half got to his feet, but Willa Pargett said, 'No, no, he's quite right.' She beamed at Ross and asked him what his name was, and he muttered it so she had to ask again, and he turned pink. She said, 'Well done, Ross, I admire your courage. And you're right. A football match is much better than a bare yard with no trees in it, and these awful breeze-block walls. Painting them pale blue doesn't help, either.' We all knew what she meant, but having her talk about the school like that was embarrassing. I mean, it was rude, really, coming from a visitor.

She went on, 'People think schoolchildren don't notice that things are ugly, but you do, of course, and so you should. The question is, what to do about it? You can't change it. If you start making your own marks on these awful walls, you'll be called vandals. So you've only two choices. You either put up with it and try not to notice, or you imagine you're somewhere else, like Ross at his football match.'

Ross was looking really pleased with himself, but Mr McInch was not enjoying it at all. He sat with his arms folded, staring grimly out of the window. I was so glad he wasn't our particular English teacher, just Head of the Department. I'd have died if we'd had him. Miss Currie was all right, though, most of the time.

Willa Pargett was going on about imagination being an important technique for a writer, and she started asking us questions again, trying to get more people to say where they'd like to be instead of here. Most of us were too embarrassed to say anything, but Shona Carfax put her hand up and said it had been nice on holiday in Lanzarote. She's too thick to be embarrassed. Jimmy Kelso, egged on by Ross, said he liked being in bed on Sunday mornings when he didn't have to do his paper round. And then Angie, looking all serious and intelligent, the way she does, said, 'Sherwood Forest.' Straight out, never asked if I'd mind or anything.

I could have killed her. After all that happened

last year, and my parents keeping it such a dead secret that we never even mentioned it among ourselves, Angie went and blurted it out in front of everyone. And the forest had been my dream, not hers, even if it *had* led to disaster. 'Angie,' I said between clenched teeth, 'shut *up*.' But she just gave me one of her cool glances, all Indian and unruffled. I wish I was brown like her, then perhaps it wouldn't show so much when I blush. As it was, I could feel myself glowing like a ring on a cooker.

'Sherwood *Forest*,' Willa Pargett said, thrilled to bits. 'Now, isn't *that* a good idea? Who's read *Robin Hood*? Or seen it on TV? Or even heard of him?' she added as only a few people looked halfway interested. 'Yes, now just think – all right, hands down – what it would be like if you were an outlaw, with a price on your head. Anyone know what that means – "a price on your head"?'

Ross was in there straight away. 'See, if someone shot you and cut your head off and took it to the King, or the Council or someone, he'd get money for it,' he said.

'That's right.' Willa Pargett nodded at him and beamed again. They were having a great time, the pair of them. 'So you'd never dare to show your face in the town, you see. The outlaws lived in the forest – the greenwood, as they called it – deep among the trees, where no one else knew the paths, and they were safe.'

I had thought it was all over, the greenwood business, left behind after what had happened, but my skin began to crawl as she spoke. That weird magic was there again, the glade with the shafts of sunlight slanting through the trees, the clink of a bridle-bit, the quiet men who could move invisibly through the wood and loose a long-shaft that would strike a man from his horse, dead before he knew it. And serve the Sheriff right for all his cruelties. But that was my world, it was private, not for Willa Pargett to talk about as if it was common property.

Angie pressed her elbow gently into my side while still looking attentively at the famous writer, and said out of the corner of her mouth, 'We'll do it for the Novel Project. Your Robin Hood thing. They'll love it.'

'You off your head?' I shrieked in a whisper.

I wasn't good at silent conversation – not like Angie. Mr McInch said loudly, 'Excuse me, Mrs Pargett – *Kelly Ferguson, I AM WATCHING YOU.*' And then he added, 'And are you *CHEWING?*'

'No!' I said, trying to sound innocent. I *was* chewing, of course – I always am.

Willa Pargett looked exasperated. 'All *right*, Mr McInch,' she said, 'I really don't mind if people chew and communicate with each other.' Miss Currie looked down at the floor. I could see she was trying not to smile.

I stopped listening after that. I was thinking about what Mum and Dad would say if they found out I'd written down what happened, for other people to read about. By the time I came to, Willa Pargett was answering the questions we'd had to prepare, like what was her favourite book, and did she like writing. I didn't ask anything.

Then we went downstairs for lunch. Angie was dead pleased with herself. 'Honest, Kelly, it's brilliant,' she said. 'We just write down all that stuff you did – change it a bit, of course, so they don't know it's you – and we've a ready-made plot.'

I said, 'No, we haven't. You're off your head, Angie. I mean, *tell* everyone? You're a total bampot, you know that?'

'They won't believe it,' Angie said, still unruffled. 'Like the woman said, the trick is to think of something fantastic and put it in a real-

7

life setting. They'll just think it's something we got from the Robin Hood story.'

I didn't answer. I couldn't.

Angie went on trying to persuade me. 'Come on, Kel, don't be daft. There's no reason why any of them should think it's you. Specially when both of us are really good at imagination.'

I said I wasn't good at anything.

'You're good at Art,' Angie said, 'and you'd be good at other things if you'd only listen to what's going on. You'd get much better marks if you did – you're quite clever, really.'

'Huh.' Try telling that to my mum, I thought.

We were moving up in the queue, towards the trays of chips and shepherd's pie. I was glad of all the clattering and talking – at least nobody was likely to overhear. 'It's all very well for you,' I said. 'You weren't involved in it. Not like I was.'

'OK,' Angie said. 'Think of something else, then.' And she smiled at the canteen woman who stood with a fish-slice in her hand, and said, 'Shepherd's pie, chips and beans, please. And a strawberry yoghurt.'

I couldn't think of anything else, not now she'd got me so agitated about Sherwood Forest and everything that had happened. I took a salad roll out of the cold cabinet.

'Don't you get sick of salad rolls?' Angie asked. 'You never have anything else.'

'Sometimes I have cheese.'

'Yes, but it's still just a roll. Don't you get hungry?'

She was having one of her nagging days. I didn't answer, just paid for the roll and put the change back in my purse for the Thin Fund. But that was private, too. The noise in the dining hall suddenly seemed overwhelming. It would have been so quiet in the greenwood, I thought.

Miss Currie was all charged up with new enthusiasm for the Novel-Writing Project after hearing Willa Pargett in the morning. 'Wasn't that terrific!' she said. 'It's such a help to get real, solid advice on how to find an idea.'

Murdo leaned forward a little and made a rude sound, then said, 'Sorry, Miss,' without looking sorry at all, and his friends did a lot of fanning and made disgusted noises, wasting a bit of time. To tell the truth, most of us were fed up with the Novel Project. There'd been such a lot of talk about how books were written, but none of it seemed to make the actual writing any easier.

When Miss Currie had got everyone more or less shut up, she said, 'Since you're working with partners, I'm going to give you ten minutes to discuss your ideas quietly and put down some notes. Nothing complicated – you don't have to start the actual book, just jot down your ideas. Remember what Mrs Pargett said – you can start with something as wild as you like, but put it into a setting that you know well, so it seems life-like.'

Angie nodded intelligently, and Miss Currie smiled at her. It was quite funny, really, the way everyone thought Angie was so marvellous. They'd never have believed she had plans to revolutionize the whole country, once she was grown-up, qualified and in the Government. She'd got it all worked out. She told me about it the first time we met, when I came to Glasgow for Gran's funeral.

People were all talking their heads off in the classroom, most of them discussing last night's telly. Under cover of the general noise, Angie said, 'How about this story, then? Are we going to do it? Or have you thought of something else?'

I could feel myself weakening. 'What if Mum and Dad see it?' I said.

'They wouldn't mind, would they?'

'Yes, they would! Specially Mum.'

'But it was all over a year ago.'

'I know, but they never even talk about it.'

'Like, they're pretending it never happened?'

'I suppose so, yes.'

'Well, that's stupid,' Angie said.

I shrugged. I didn't know if it was stupid or not and, either way, there was nothing I could do about it.

Angie said there'd be nothing for them to fuss about, anyway. 'We'll change the story,' she said. 'Have a happy ending. I mean, it's *fiction*, Kel. Your big chance to be a real hero.'

Maybe Mum and Dad would never see it, I thought. There was no real reason why they should. 'Oh, all right,' I said. 'We'll go for it.' I could always bail out if it got really embarrassing.

'Great,' said Angie. She picked up her pen and wrote, in neat capital letters at the top of her page, *The Sherwood Hero*. Then underlined it, using a ruler.

CHAPTER 2

Angie came home with me after school. She nearly always did, since she lived in the flat next door. We thought it would be great if there was a connecting door so we could pop in and out without all that trekking down the stairs to the street and up again, but we couldn't get anyone to take the idea seriously.

There was nobody in except Granda. He was always there, because he had arthritis and he couldn't get out without someone to help him down the steps. You had to carry one of his sticks while he leaned on the other one and held on to the banister. He said, 'Hi, pet. You had a good day? Hi, Angie.'

'Hello, Mr Ferguson.'

'We'd this writer came to see us,' I told him. 'Willa Pargett.'

'Never heard of her. Are youse wantin' a cup of tea?' He was shuffling about in the kitchen, unwrapping a pack of currant buns while the kettle boiled.

'Yes, please.' Once he'd had his cuppa and

talked for a bit, he'd settle with his paper, and Angie and I could leave him to it.

'So what did she say, this writer woman?'

'Just . . . about using our imaginations.' Suddenly, this was dangerous territory. Granda was all right, though – he'd always been on my side. But, all the same, I wanted time to think about it before I told him what we were up to.

'Imagination – aye, well, that's the stuff,' he said. 'You know what Einstein said? "Imagination is more important than knowledge." Now, there's a thing. See, if you canny imagine what it is you want to know, you'll never get knowin' it.'

'I suppose that's how he thought of relativity,' Angie suggested. Fancy knowing about relativity, I ask you. But she's like that.

'So he did, right enough,' Granda said. Then he looked at me and said, 'You're awfu' quiet, Kelly.'

'Am I?' It was no good trying to keep anything secret from Granda, he always seemed to know. 'I was just – thinking.'

'Were you.' It wasn't a question. He poured out three mugs of tea, and ladled two spoonfuls of sugar into his own and stirred it untidily. 'Did yez bring the paper?'

'There you go.' We always collected his *Evening*

Times from the shop by the bus stop.

'Ah. Good lassies.' He lowered himself into his chair and propped his sticks against the table, then unfolded the paper. It was our signal that we could go.

My room has this turret window in the corner, with a horseshoe-shaped seat in it, so that's where Angie and I always sit. You can see out across all the roofs and the railway line and the football pitch that's lit up at night, right over to the hills. That's the nice thing about Glasgow, the way the hills are so near. It was only a year ago when I came here, and it seemed really strange after London. Sort of raw, as if the wind brought a smell of sheep and bracken. And everyone getting into conversations, whether they knew each other or not, though they all talked to each other as if they did.

Angie got straight down to business. 'We'll need to work out how to change things,' she said. 'Names, for a start. Who are you going to be?'

I didn't know, of course. I hadn't thought about it.

'I'll be Jasmine,' Angie said.

'*Jasmine!*'

'What's funny about that? I've an auntie called Jasmine.'

'Oh. Well, I suppose you could be Jazz for short.' I couldn't imagine Angie being called Jasmine. Might as well be Hyacinth.

Angie thought about it, licking stickiness off her fingers from the currant bun. I hadn't had one. Ever since I started the Thin Fund, I'd gone off things like buns, even if I didn't have to buy them.

'But we'll have to stop thinking of the book people as you and me,' she said. 'They're just characters. What's the other one going to be called?'

'Erm – Kirsty?'

Angie wrinkled her nose, not fancying it. 'Too near to Kelly,' she said.

'Oh. Yes, I suppose it is.' Why hadn't I noticed? I couldn't think of this girl as anyone but me, that was the trouble.

'Some crazy name would be best,' Angie said. 'The madder it is, the better.'

''Cos it seems more unlikely.' I got the point. 'My brother used to know a girl called Tuesday.' Big brother Ian, four hundred miles away now, working in London. How I missed him.

'Who on earth would call their kid Tuesday? You'd never know if you were talking about a person or a date. No, we want something with a silly sound, not a silly meaning.'

'Hollyhock,' I said, still thinking about flowers. 'Honeysuckle, Bluebell.'

'Jezebel. Hey, that would be a laugh, Jazz and Jez.'

'Brilliant!' I said. Not that I thought it was all that funny, but I wanted Angie to think I was trying.

Angie wrote the names down in her jotter and said, 'Right, that's the names settled. Now, what are we going to do about writing it? Take turns to write a chapter each, like Miss Currie suggested? Or both write our own version and then combine them? That might be best, then we can use all the good bits and scrap the rest.'

'I don't want to do a chapter each,' I said. After all, whatever Angie said about changing the story into fiction, it was still about something that had happened to me, and I wanted to be pretty careful about what got written down. Angie hadn't been so involved. As she said at the time, a person who is going to be Prime Minister one day has to be careful not to get a criminal record. It wasn't that I didn't trust her, but . . .

'You don't trust me,' Angie said.

I blushed. We knew each other too well to

pretend. 'It's not *you*,' I said, 'it's just . . . I'd like to be sure what gets put into this novel and what doesn't. I mean, people might read it.' The thought made me feel terrified all over again, and I said, 'Look, Angie, honestly, I think we ought to do something else.'

Angie thought about it. 'The only thing is,' she said, 'Miss Currie's dead keen on it. If we try to change it, she'll want to know why. And we can't say it's because you feel bad about it – that would be like announcing to everyone that it really happened.'

She was right, of course. Miss Currie had read Angie's notes out to the class during the afternoon's lesson, all about how this girl had got so keen on the Robin Hood story, she'd decided to carry on where he left off, robbing the rich to feed the poor. A lot of people had laughed, but everyone thought it was dead clever. We got side-tracked by Murdo, when he started on about being lifted by the police for nicking stuff off a building site, and how there's no handles on the inside of the rear doors of police cars, so you can't get out. Murdo didn't mind a bit about people knowing. But then, crime was probably going to be his career, so he wouldn't be bothered. Nobody thought Angie's rob-the-rich girl was me, though, I had to admit that.

Angie clicked her fingers, suddenly struck by a new idea. 'Tell you what – why don't we do it like a telly interview? I'll be the reporter, asking you the questions, and you can say whatever you want. Or for a newspaper, even better. My dad says they're mostly fiction anyway, because they get things wrong all the time.'

'I thought people could sue newspapers if they printed lies,' I said, and Angie sighed as if I was being particularly stupid.

'If the paper says you've done all sorts of wonderful things, you're not going to mind, are you?' she pointed out. 'Even if it *is* lies. You'll only sue if you don't *like* the lies. No, listen, Kel, if we do it that way, then you're in charge of what gets written. That's OK, isn't it?'

'Suppose so.'

'I think it's great,' Angie said happily. 'You get to do all the hard work, making up the story, and all I have to do is write it down.'

Then I thought of a snag. 'What am I going to do while you're scribbling away at the story? We're both supposed to write something, and I can't just sit there doing nothing after I've told you what to put down.'

'Uh,' said Angie, stumped for a moment. 'Well,

doodle about with a Plot Diagram or something. Write some Atmosphere.'

'Perhaps I could do some illustrations,' I said.

'There you go, then. Great. Miss Currie won't come near us much, anyway, not with Kevin and Murdo and all that lot. She never does. And that's fine, because I like to get things all sorted out properly before anyone sees them.'

'I don't like people seeing what I've done at all,' I said.

Angie argued, as usual. 'Yes, you do. What about your Art stuff? There are always pictures of yours on the wall.'

'That's different.' Art doesn't use words. I quite like words, they're better than numbers, but the trouble is, everyone uses them, so there are these rules about what's right or wrong. With Art, you can make up your own rules. Angie says she likes other people's rules, because then you can decide if you're going to obey them or not, and why, but I can never understand why they made them in the first place, and I don't really want to find out. But I didn't go into all that.

Angie was adding bits to her notes. She read out what she had written, although I'd heard most of it before.

' "*The Sherwood Hero* – a novel about a girl

who thinks Robin Hood was right. She thinks things should be organized better, so rich people have to give some of their money to help the poor. She decides to be an outlaw like Robin Hood and do it herself, only it is quite difficult and she has to be very brave. The book will be about how she gets some money and gives it away. In the end, the person she gets it from thinks she was right to do it and that is why she is a hero." That's as far as I've got. What did you put?'

'Nothing much,' I said. My jotter was all tattooed with ballpoint doodlings, and I'd only written one line. It said, 'This is going to be a story about the greenwood, only it is set in Glasgow.'

'Well, that's all right,' Angie said when I read it out. 'Now we just need the details. What she actually did.'

I froze. 'Angie, I *can't*. If we start with me coming to Glasgow last summer after Gran died, they'll all know.'

Angie sighed again. 'Don't be daft,' she said. 'That's got nothing to do with it. Think about this girl called Jez. She's not you, she's someone else. She does different things.'

'But *what*?' I said, agonized. I hadn't realized

20

how difficult this writing business was going to be.

'Well, anything. She could have been in Glasgow all the time. Maybe her parents run a café or something – come on, Kel, you're usually good at this sort of thing. You're being stupid.'

She was right. I felt like a frightened horse, all quivering muscles and twitching skin, wanting to run away, not stop and think, just go. I wasn't usually like that. But then, school wasn't usually like this. It had reached out a long tentacle, right into my bedroom, touching on the things I dreamed about and tried not to think about. 'Maybe we could start with her reading *Robin Hood*,' I said. It sounded pretty feeble.

Angie nodded and said, 'We'll need to do that, anyway, or half of them won't know what we're on about.'

'Yes, they will,' I said. 'Everyone's heard of Robin Hood.' But I had started to see the girl who was reading the book. 'We could make her very unheroic,' I said. 'With mousy hair like mine, only tied back neatly, with escaping wisps. They always have escaping wisps in books. And she could be small and skinny, with big glasses, and very quiet and well-behaved in school.'

'A right wee sook,' Angie said, using the

Glasgow word for someone who sucks up to the teacher.

'Even worse than you.'

'Oh, thanks a lot!'

Anyway, we got going on the homework Miss Currie had set, writing up more notes on the Project, and I put down what Jez looked like, and how she was reading about the Sheriff of Nottingham, who was so cruel that he'd have your hand chopped off if you killed one of the King's deer to feed your starving family. I got angry about it all over again as I wrote, even though it had all happened a year ago and I was supposed to have forgotten about it. And Mum seemed as close as if she'd been looking over my shoulder, reading the words. 'Don't give me that about robbing the rich,' her voice said in my ear. 'Stealing is a crime. Anyone who steals is a criminal.' I was a criminal.

I stopped writing. Mum had not been there, it was only my imagination. But I couldn't see the girl called Jez any longer. There was just me, sitting here with the shakes.

Angie looked up and said, 'How're you doing?'

'Terrible,' I said. I passed her my jotter, and she read what I had written, then handed it back and said, 'Great. I like all that about the King's deer.' Then she pushed her own jotter back into her school bag and dropped her pen in after it. 'I'll have to go,' she said. 'It's my turn to help with tea.' There were a lot of them in her family, so they had a rota system for the jobs. 'Dream up something about how Jez does the robbery bit, right?' she added. 'Then I'll interview you and write it down. See you in the morning, OK?'

'OK,' I said, and wondered how it was that I sounded so normal.

CHAPTER 3

When Angie had gone, I went on sitting in the window seat. I didn't want to go on brooding over what had happened, but it's surprisingly difficult to pull your mind away from something that's nagging at you. Mum and Dad had made it very clear that I was not supposed to think about it, and up until now I'd managed to keep it tucked away, but this horrible Project was dragging it all up again. Even though we were going to turn it into something quite different, I still had to remember all the details. I mean, you can't make something different unless you know what it's different *from*.

The hardest thing was trying to work out how it all started. I'd liked Robin Hood for ages, of course, but that was separate from actually deciding to do something about it. Certainly I hadn't thought of anything like that until I came to Glasgow, so I could leave all the London years out of it. That made things simpler. There was nothing much I wanted to remember about London, anyway. I was just a kid, not allowed out on my own because Mum said it was dangerous. She took me to and from school. At home, I read a lot of books and had bad dreams about fire and a weird place that scared me. Mum and Dad thought the dreams might be because of the books, so one of them always came with me to the library, to make sure I didn't borrow anything unsuitable. I never got to read any ghost stories or thrillers, and they weren't even happy about Tolkien, only my class teacher said it was all right, we were Doing it. I didn't think my nightmares were about books, though. They were always about people who watched, and about dogs, and these fires burning – I pushed the thought of them away. Sitting in the window seat on that September afternoon, I still found those dreams frightening.

The Robin Hood business must have started at Gran's funeral, really. It was last June, just over a year ago. I'd been to Glasgow before, of course, lots of times, to see Gran and Granda and spend holidays with them. Ian used to come, too, before he left school and started work at the Gas Board and met Susan. I missed him so much when he left home and went off to live with her, it seemed terribly quiet at mealtimes without his jokes and absurdities.

Susan couldn't get off work for the funeral, she's a teacher and it was exam time, but I didn't mind her not being there. Ian came, and that was great. He drove us up in his car, because he'd not long passed his test and he was dead keen on driving. We stopped twice at motorway cafés, and he and I had a go at the game machines. There was a race-track one where you could have a steering-wheel each, and I beat him. He was furious.

The funeral was awful. I'd never been to one before, and it wasn't a bit what I'd expected. There was no churchyard and no grave, just this white concrete crematorium with a triangular-shaped chimney that pretended it was a tower. And inside, there were rows of red plastic benches that puffed when you sat down on them, as if they were full of air.

I know it sounds silly, but I'd imagined a long procession in some country place, with the coffin carried on men's shoulders between tall trees, and the sky very pale and clear. It was dampish, as if it had been raining. Funny, that, the way I saw it as if I was down the slope a bit, looking up at this procession moving against the sky, with rooks going up from the bare trees – yes, they were bare, things like what month it is don't come into dreams – and I wasn't part of it, I just watched from down the hill, with these rooks flying about like scraps of burned paper, and I felt sad, but I loved it, too, because it was so beautiful.

The real thing wasn't beautiful at all. The hymns were printed on plastic sheets that could be wiped, like café table mats. There's always this gap between the way I think things are going to be and the way they really are, and it's nearly always disappointing.

Everyone came back to this flat afterwards, and the men stood about with drinks, all of them in suits and black ties, talking about business and cars and Dad being made redundant. The women had aprons over their best dresses, and went in and out of the kitchen with garlic bread and rice salad and ham, putting all the stuff on the big table in the front room next to this one. This used to be Gran's and Granda's bedroom then. Gran died in here. She went for a wee rest, Granda said, and he came in a couple of hours later with a cup of tea for her, and there she was. She'd had what they called a massive heart attack. That was always the word, 'massive'. Not just big or drastic. She wasn't fat or anything, not the sort of person who looks, as Dad says, 'like a heart attack about to happen'. She was a skinny little thing, really. But she did like her cigarettes. Mum said it was a good way to go and, after all, she *was* nearly eighty. Mum and Dad thought I wouldn't want this room, not after Gran died in it, but I didn't mind. Gran was lovely, and if her ghost is about, that's OK by me. She was like a little rough terrier, the way she kept Granda in order. 'Ye great daft lump,' she used to say, although she barely came to his shoulder, and he'd look down at her and say, 'Mind yer manners, woman' – but they were great together, the pair of them.

It was awful seeing Granda so quiet at the funeral, because he's not a bit quiet usually. He sat in that wooden chair of his with the carved arms, and he looked really old, as if there was nothing of him under his navy blue suit. He answered anyone who spoke to him, and even smiled a bit, but as soon as they went away, he'd be looking at nothing again.

That's where I met Angie, at the funeral. She came over and offered me a crisp – Mum had put them in bowls – and said, 'Are you upset about your Gran?' I thought it was a bit rude, coming out with a personal question like that, but I found out afterwards that Glasgow people don't worry so much about saying the proper thing, not like in London, they just get straight to the point. Angie looked terrific. She was wearing a black dress with a short skirt and a big roll-neck collar. Mum wouldn't let me wear all black, she said it was too heavy for someone my age and Gran wouldn't have liked it, but I think she would, she always dressed up if she was going somewhere special. So I had my black school skirt on, and black tights and shoes, but with a grey-and-white-striped sweatshirt, and I felt all wrong, all mousy and lumpy, specially compared with Angie, who was Indian and very composed, with her black hair cut short at the back but in a heavy fringe that came down to her eyebrows. She wore these silver earrings, too, very intricate, and when I said they looked great, she said, 'Why don't you get your ears pierced? Then people can give you earrings for birthdays and things.' I said I didn't think Mum would let me, and Angie looked surprised. 'They're your ears,' she'd said. But then, Angie's mother wore wonderful earrings, too, and lots of bangles, and a sari. I couldn't imagine my mother in earrings. And I certainly couldn't imagine asking her if I could get my ears pierced.

Anyway, I told Angie, yes, I was upset about Gran, but I was more sorry for Granda, being left on his own, and Angie said how her mother had been bringing food round for him since Gran died, but he'd hardly eat anything. And when Mrs Khan (Angie's mum) had suggested she should clean the windows, he wouldn't have it. He said it would seem all wrong, seeing another woman standing on a chair when Gran had always done it. And then he had cried, Angie's mother had said, for the first time, and she wished she hadn't suggested it, even though it's a good thing to cry and get things off your chest.

You could see nobody had cleaned the windows. The sunshine of the summer day could hardly struggle through the grimy glass. The whole flat was pretty grubby, even though Mrs Khan had done a great job in the kitchen. But you could see the cobwebs stretched like hammocks across the corners of the sitting room, at the top of the long, faded curtains, and the bathroom had ghastly dark green paint, and the plaster was falling off the ceiling. I'd never noticed before how tacky it all was. I thought Gran must have stopped being able to cope with it in the past year. And Granda couldn't do anything because of his arthritis. Neither of them would have dreamed of asking for help, though.

Angie suddenly said, 'Is that right, you're coming here to stay?'

I was a bit stunned that she knew about it. Mum and Dad had been discussing the idea of leaving London, because of Dad's firm going bust, and Ian had been saying in the car on the way up to Glasgow how the flat was far too big for Granda to manage on his own, and how he'd need someone to look after him or else he'd have to go into a home, and he'd hate that. But I hadn't listened, not really. I'd got out of the habit of listening to that sort of thing, because if I said anything, Mum and Dad would say it was nothing for me to worry about. They always worried about me worrying. All I knew was that Mum had asked if I'd mind going to a different school, but I knew I'd be changing schools anyway, because I was due to leave the Primary. But I didn't know she meant for certain that we'd be coming to Glasgow. I hoped we would, though. I was secretly excited about it, because I always liked it better than London. I loved the smell of the air, and the way women called each other 'hen'.

So I told Angie I thought we might be coming here, and she said that was great, and she hoped I'd be coming to her school, because we could go in on the bus together.

Angie wasn't a bit like the Asian girls who'd been at my school in London. Most of them were very quiet in their brightly coloured long tunics and trousers, and only talked to each other, but Angie explained afterwards that her family had been in Glasgow for over a hundred years, so it was hardly surprising that she didn't sound Indian. She didn't sound very broad Glasgow, either, not like Granda, but she sounded Scottish. And when she wasn't in school clothes, she wore jeans and big T-shirts that she mostly filched from her brothers, and brilliant plastic earrings that would have sent Mr McInch into a fit. I really did rather envy her the earrings. Her father always looked very smart, in a dark suit, but then, he was an accountant. Mrs Khan wore saris because she said they were more comfortable. I thought they looked wonderful. I still do. I wish I could wear them, but for someone as fair and pink as me, it would be ridiculous. I don't much like the look of myself, I never have.

It was at the funeral that Angie told me she was going to be the prime minister when she grew up. After going to university, she said, and getting herself elected as an MP. 'If we're to be friends, you might as well know,' she said in a matter-of-fact way. Thank goodness I didn't laugh. With

Granda sitting there staring into space, things weren't very funny anyway, but I had the feeling that Angie would walk off and never speak to me again if I laughed. So I just said, 'Well, somebody's got to do it.' And she said, 'Dead right.'

Mum came past with a bowl of lettuce and said, 'Oh, good, you're getting to know each other,' and smiled at Angie. Angie smiled back, but as soon as Mum had gone, she asked me if I was an only child. I was a bit offended, because everyone thinks only children are spoilt, so I said, 'That's my brother over there with the striped shirt, talking to those men.' And Angie said, 'Is he your only one?'

I don't know what it is about Angie, but when she's around, I always seem to find myself doing things I hadn't expected to do. At the funeral, we'd only known each other for about ten minutes, and I found myself telling her something I'd never told anyone else, about how Mum had had a baby in between Ian and me, but it had died. Mum and Dad had never told me about it, but Ian did, and I'd always felt that it was a dark secret, and yet I told it to someone who had only just stopped being a stranger. I still don't know why I was so sure it would be all right. Angie wasn't even much concerned. She just nodded and said, 'I thought it must be something like that, with your brother being so much older.' Then she said, 'What are you going to be? When you're grown up, I mean.'

I said I hadn't decided. We'd had this visit to a sweet factory when I was still at the Primary, because Mrs Parslow thought it would be interesting for us, and afterwards we went into a big room and got given packets of sweets, and a man talked about working in the factory, and how it was never too early to start thinking about jobs, because it made you realize the value of your education, and how you mustn't waste time. The funny thing was, it made me want to go away somewhere and waste lots of time, because it was so awful to think of standing at a moving belt, stuffing packets of sweets into little cardboard boxes. But Angie didn't mean that sort of job. She frowned and said, 'Don't you have some idea of what you *really* might be? I mean, even if it seems totally ridiculous.'

You couldn't get anything much more ridiculous than wanting to be the prime minister, I thought. After that, my own little dream was going to sound pretty tame. But all the same, it was only after several sweaty-palmed seconds that I knew I really *was* going to tell her. Even then, it was difficult. Angie was watching me. 'I won't laugh,' she said. 'Promise. *You* didn't.'

Yes, that's where it began, in that hot room with its smells of whisky and sausage rolls and salt-and-vinegar crisps. It's our sitting room now, but it seemed so different on the day of the funeral, with all those people in it, talking so loudly that Angie and I could only just hear each other. I told her about the greenwood, and the secret army of people who lived there, and when she was about to say she knew all about that, it was just Robin Hood, I got to the meeting in the glade between the trees, with the horses shifting quietly and the sun coming down through the dappled leaves, and the faces turned to listen. And it was me they listened to. I'd never wished it to be me. But there was no choice. I was Robin. The faces looked to me, expectantly, and I had to outline the plan of ambush and attack, so that one day, we might drive away the Sheriff and his paid soldiers, and live in our own homes again.

Angie listened, and didn't interrupt. 'I know it's not a career,' I said. 'I mean, there's no green-wood or Guy of Gisborne any more, or horses or long-bows. But I'd like to do something – I don't know what. Something to make things better for people.'

I knew my face was scarlet. I stared down at the glass of orange juice I was holding. It was almost finished, but I hadn't liked to ask for any more. Angie wasn't a bit embarrassed, though. 'You're like me, then!' she said. She sounded quite excited. 'You want things to be fair. See, when I'm Prime Minister, I'll give everyone a living allowance, right from the day they're born. Not a lot, but enough to live on. Then anyone who wants to work can earn extra, but if you're at home with children, or unemployed, you've still got some money. It saves all this hassle with the DSS, and people getting accused of cheating if they do a bit of work on the side.'

I didn't know what she was on about. I understand it now, and it's a really good idea, but nobody had told me anything about unemployment then.

That's as far as we got, because Mrs Khan came in and clapped her hands, which made all her bangles jingle, and said, 'There's food in the next room, folks.' Everyone converged round Granda, trying to help him out of his chair, but he put his hand out to me and said, 'C'mon, Kelly. It's you an' me, pal.' And he levered himself up, leaning on his stick, and I took his other hand, and we went through to the dining room together. I didn't get to talk to Angie again until after we'd moved to Glasgow.

CHAPTER 4

I don't quite know why I'm writing all these things down, the memories and nightmares and the way they all came surging up because of the horrible Project and Willa Pargett's visit. It's partly Granda's fault, because he thought it was a good idea and started helping me, but it's more to do with wanting to get all these things sorted out and pinned down.

Did you ever play Blind Man's Buff? I used to hate that game, the way you get poked and prodded by things you can't see, and when you make a grab for one of them, they all dance away out of reach and you've caught nothing. It's like that with things that give you the heebies, you can't get a good look at them.

Now I've started, of course, it's difficult to stop. I get so caught up in the remembering that it seems to be happening all over again, and I don't know if anyone who might be reading this could make any sense of it. My trouble is, the things I'm thinking about can be much more real to me than what's actually going on right now. Maybe if this ever gets to be a proper book, the remembered bits could be in bigger print or something. Miss Currie would laugh at the idea of me writing a book. She still thinks I'm a hopeless case, you can see that. Even though I'm better than I used to be.

Anyway, on the morning after Willa Pargett's visit, Angie and I met at the bus stop as usual. It was right between Angie's entry to the flats and mine, so it was dead handy. Mum would frown at me using the word 'dead', she says I'm getting very Glasgow, but I don't think I am, really. It's just that the way people speak here used to sound strange, but it doesn't any more. And some of the words are – well – dead handy.

When we'd got on the bus, Angie said, 'Have you thought what to put next?'

No, I'd not thought. Not about the writing, anyway. But Angie wasn't put off. She fished out her jotter and said, 'Right. Interview time.'

'Pete's sake, Angie, not here.'

'How no'?' she said, sounding like Granda for a minute. 'It's better here than at school. And if we do it now, we won't have to talk about it in Miss Currie's lesson, just write it down.'

Angie was so *sensible*. I said, 'Oh, all right, then,' and she switched on a television smile and asked her first question. 'How did it all begin, Jez?'

'That's exactly what I've been trying to work out,' I said, not being Jez at all.

Angie rolled her eyes and tried again. 'You'd always liked Robin Hood, hadn't you,' she said, still interviewing. 'But what started you thinking you might do something like he did?'

I frowned, desperately trying to think of something. We'd moved to Glasgow pretty soon after the funeral, then there had been a week or two of nothing much, before school started. I'd helped Mum with her blitz on the flat, and taken Granda out sometimes, to change his library books.

'It might have been just some little thing,' Angie prompted.

'I took my grandfather to the library,' I said, trying to be Jez, the girl we were writing about. But I couldn't be her, it was just me, remembering.

'Yes?'

Granda had crabbed his way down the stairs, with me beside him, and out through the entry, and I'd given him his other stick once we were safely on the pavement. I'd liked the way there was grass growing in between the great stone paving slabs.

'I carried his bag of books,' I said. And he'd got on fine, in a hop-and-swing sort of way, lurching along on his two sticks.

'Keep going,' Angie said.

'Well, you know what the library's like, dead grand, with those steps up to the door—'

'Is that the Carnegie library – the main one?'

'That's right. There's a ramp for wheelchairs, but he was all for heading up the steps, he's that obstinate.'

'Then what?'

'I made him go up the ramp, and he was a bit out of breath when he got to the top, but he wouldn't admit it, of course. He stood there, panting a bit, and looked up at the name carved in the stone above the door. "Andrew Carnegie," he said. "His father was a weaver, Kelly, back in the old days when folks were starvin'." And then he told me all about how the Carnegies had gone to America, and Andrew had started work in a cotton factory when he was only thirteen. "No' much older than you, Kelly," he said.'

I stopped. I was back on that day. The sun had been so warm.

'You might be on to something there,' Angie said. 'Go on.'

'Well, he told me how Andrew Carnegie got

rich and came back to Scotland and built all these libraries and universities and things. He said it was because he wanted to use up his money before he died. And when we got inside, he hauled me over to a great fat encyclopaedia and looked up Carnegie and read bits out. "Listen to this, Kelly, what the man said – *A man who dies rich dies disgraced.* Some statement, eh?" '

'So it is,' Angie agreed. 'That's it, isn't it?'

'What?'

'The beginning. There's this famous man saying it's wrong to be greedy, you should share.'

She was right. 'Amazing,' I said. 'Problem solved.' It was a nice feeling, like fitting a piece into a jigsaw. I was still remembering the library, with Granda browsing along his dusty old biographies and me sitting on the windowsill, looking out. 'Hey, Angie, I saw you that morning – I never told you.'

'Did you?' she said, interested. 'How? What was I doing?'

'You were walking along, outside, with some other people. Sylvia, and Peter Carrick and a couple of other boys. I didn't know any of them then. I really envied you, having all those friends.'

'You should have banged on the window or shouted out or something,' Angie said. 'We'd have come in.' She always made things sound so simple. 'Anyway,' she went on, 'what happened next?'

'I was a bit bored, really. I'm not much good in libraries. I liked it when I was little, and you could sit in a wooden railway train and look at picture books, but I never know what to get now. So I'd just picked up a book of photos of old Glasgow, because I thought Granda would like telling me all about it. He had an armful, of course, and when they'd been checked out, he wanted to go and have a cup of tea. "An' a sticky," he said.'

'He does love his cakes,' Angie agreed. 'So where did you go?'

'I can't remember what it was called. There's a café just down the road – it's a room behind a baker's shop. We had Millionaire's shortbread, "Carnegie shortbread", he said.' It used to be one of my favourites, with the chocolate on top, and the pepperminty bit, but that was before I started the Thin Fund, of course. Before I got into such a mess. But I wouldn't think about that. Not yet. 'He insisted on carrying his own tea from the counter,' I told Angie, 'so of course he spilt it in the saucer.'

'I'm not writing all that down,' Angie said. 'It's irrelevant.'

'Is it? Sorry.'

'Well, I mean, we haven't got much time. We'll be at school in a minute. What did you talk about in the café?'

'Books.'

'What books?'

'He wanted to know why I'd not got a book to read. Photos were all very well, he said, but you couldny beat a real good read. And he started asking what books I liked.'

'And you said—'

'*Robin Hood*,' we chorused, and fell about laughing.

'There you go, then,' Angie said when we had recovered a bit. 'That's the beginning.'

'We can't use Granda!' I shrieked. 'He's *real*!'

'Make him into something else, then,' said Angie. 'What did he say, anyway, when you told him about you-know-who?'

'He thought it was great.'

Angie was pushing her jotter back into her bag. I saw the school building through the window. 'We could make him into a teacher or something,' she said.

'Teachers aren't like that. Not mad enough.'

'Friend, then. Someone Jez's father knows.'

We got off the bus and went in through the

gate and across the tarmac yard, but I was still in the café with Granda, like rerunning a film. So this is the bit that ought to be in different type, if it ever gets printed.

He told me they used to call Robin the Wolf's Head, because he ran through the forest like a wolf, with a price on his head. And we'd sat in the café, full of enthusiasm for the life of the outlaw in the greenwood. Granda had held out a straight left arm and fitted an imaginary arrow to the bow-string, and drawn it back. 'For the Sheriff,' he said, narrow-eyed. And then he let it go. And I said darkly, 'Guy of Gisborne. A cross-bow bolt.'

We talked a long time that morning, in the café with its beds of artificial plants between the back-to-back bench seats, and its pink fluorescent lights. He asked me about London, and whether it was true that there were so many people begging and sleeping in shop doorways, and I said yes, it was, but I felt sort of guilty, because Mum didn't like me to think about things like that, she thought it wasn't nice for me to know about them. She was probably right, because they made me feel strangely sick and shaky.

Granda brooded about it for a bit, then he looked at me and said, 'Ye know what, Kelly, I could be tempted.' And when I asked him what he meant, he said, 'The time's coming when we'll need to take the law into our own hands.' ('Wir own hands' is what he really said, being Glasgow.) 'Get some decency back. These poor folk livin' in the streets as if they were rats. Rob the rich and feed the poor, aye, so we should. I tell ye, we've lost wir courage. If I wisni' so bloody old — 'scuse me — I'd do it.' And he looked so fierce and forlorn, sitting there with his two sticks, I put my hand over his and said, 'Don't you worry. I'll do it. I promise.' And a shiver ran over my skin. I had taken a vow, and it was already frightening.

'So ye will, lassie,' he said, and sandwiched my hand with his other one, rough and warm. 'So ye will.' But I can see now, he never thought I meant it, he just thought I'd do something when I grew up, like Angie. We had to go home, because we knew Mum would have dinner ready. He heaved himself to his feet and said, 'See what Maid Marian's cooked up for us, eh? Roast haunch of venison.' And we went out, with me carrying his bag of books again.

I knew I couldn't blame Granda, though. All that morning at school, I thought about making him that promise, and wondered why I meant it so passionately. I mean, it was a weird thing for someone of not quite thirteen to think she could do. That's what people kept asking me afterwards, 'Whatever were you thinking of?' Angie was asking the same thing, in a way. It was all Willa Pargett's fault. If she hadn't come and stirred up all this enthusiasm for the Novel Project, I'd have gone on trying to forget the whole thing. As it was, my mind was on the boil.

The trouble with school is, there's no time to think. You're always supposed to be doing something. But I've got this technique of propping my head on my hand and looking as if I've just paused in the middle of writing something, and if there's not too much noise going on, I can get off into quite a long bit of thinking that way. Angie had got me going about Granda, and I didn't want to stop.

When we first came to the flat he was still a bit quiet, but he started to cheer up after a week or two, and we got into those argumentative mealtimes that happen all the time now. It was the book I'd got from the library that started him off. He'd been looking through it, even though he didn't approve of my choice, and he'd come across a picture of men marching with banners, just as Mum called us in for tea, and he came to the table full

47

of talk about Black Friday. 'Thirty-first of January 1919,' he said, spearing a chip. 'Fifty-three people mown down in George Square. That was for marchin', Kelly.'

Dad said times had changed, and it was no use marching any more, it was every man for himself. Granda clapped a hand to his forehead and said with closed eyes, 'God forgive ye, boy. That a son of mine should say a thing like that.'

I said, 'Were you there, Granda? On Black Friday?' and Mum said he couldn't have been, he was only a year old. Granda said, 'In my mother's arms, lassie. Aye, in my mother's arms.' And Dad rolled his eyes and said, 'Here we go again.' But I hadn't heard any of it before, and I thought it was great, and Granda got going about the Red Clydesiders, who were protesting about how bad things were in Glasgow, with the shipyards laid up. 'An' they made the Government listen,' he said, 'an' after that the yards got going again. Job number 534. You know what ship that was, Kelly?'

I shook my head, but Dad said, 'The Queen Mary.'

'Three red funnels, she had,' Granda told me. 'I can see them now.' And he marked the three sloping lines in the air with his knife.

Mum said, 'Don't let your fish get cold,' and he ate

a mouthful, brooding, and I looked at him, and he
winked. You an' me, pal.

Angie wasn't happy. When it came to English, she sat frowning over her jotter, turning the pages of notes she had made in the bus that morning, and looking dissatisfied. 'If you don't want us to use all this stuff about you and your Granda going to the library, I don't know what to put,' she said.

Luckily, Miss Currie was still in Discussion mode, so it didn't matter too much that we were arguing. Everyone else had been told to 'talk quietly in pairs', so they were shouting their heads off. Angie and I wrangled on about whether we could include Granda, and if not, who we'd turn him into, and at last I got fed up with the whole thing, and said, 'If you really want to know, it all started at the launderette.'

Angie stared at me for a minute, black eyes under the heavy fringe of black hair, then said, 'Well, why didn't you *say* so?'

'Because I've only just thought of it,' I shouted, then added, 'sorry. But I mean, the launderette was just us. Not Granda.'

'You mean, when you tried to give some money to that alky.'

'Yes.'

'There you go, then,' Angie said, looking happier. 'That's a really OK start. Jazz and Jez in the launderette. Or maybe just Jez,' she added.

Perhaps it was a bit mean, but I said, 'You're going to be in this as well. It was your idea to use it.' And I quoted her own words – 'I mean, it's *fiction*, Ange.'

'Oh, all right,' she said huffily. I could see she was thinking the whole thing over. 'It *is* sort of difficult, isn't it?' she said. 'Being in it yourself.'

'Dead difficult,' I said.

We looked at each other carefully, then grinned. 'Jazz and Jez,' I said, and Angie nodded. 'Not us.' We almost shook hands on it, but that would have been going a bit far. Then we started to write about the launderette.

CHAPTER 5

I didn't get very far. Writing was such hard work. I hadn't thought of it then as something private, that you can do for yourself – it was just an exercise for other people to look at and mark. I hated it. There were so many difficulties. To start with, I couldn't decide how to spell the laun/lawn derett/dret/drette, and then I got stuck on wondering if Jezz ought to have two zeds so that it looked like Jazz, and whether those were the right names, anyway. Or whether we ought to have made them boys instead of girls. I wanted to ask Angie, but she was writing away as if she was getting paid a pound a word, and I didn't like to disturb her. So I chewed my pen and did the head-leaning bit, and went off into remembering that summer morning last year.

It had all started with Angie coming round to ask if I'd go to Tesco's with her. Mum looked a bit nose-out-of-joint, and said she could have done with a hand, taking the stuff to the launderette – Dad hadn't plumbed the washing machine in at that stage. Fancy Gran and Granda managing all that time without one. Anyway, Angie said, no problem, there was a launderette just by Tesco's, we could drop the stuff in and get the messages, and uplift it on the way back. Mum and I both blinked a bit, but I knew 'messages' meant shopping, and I soon clicked that you uplift things in Scotland rather than pick them up.

So off we went with these great bags of washing, and when we got to the launderette, the woman asked if we wanted a Service Wash. I was going to say we did, because Mum had given me the money for it, but Angie was already ramming things into machines. 'No, we'll do it,' she said. She was very decided about it, and pointed out that there were other things I could do with that money. I said it wasn't my money, it was Mum's, and we had quite an argument about it. Angie said, 'If she was going to pay someone to do that job, she might as well pay you as anyone else.' Her uncle always paid them if they helped in his shop, she said, even Moti who was only eleven although he looked older, and her dad thought that was right, and he was an accountant, so he should know.

We weren't like that in our family. Mum and Dad had always given me pocket money, but if I helped in the house, it was just because I ought to, and there was no question of getting paid for it.

Anyway, once the washing was in the machines, we went off to Tesco's and loaded up this trolley, because the Khans got through a lot of stuff, there being so many of them. Mum had asked me if I could remember to get her a lettuce and some teabags and a bottle of turps, so I went through the checkout first with just my three things, and Angie behind me with the trolley.

And the woman who went before me left her purse.

How could I have forgotten? That was something we could put in the Novel, because it was nothing to do with me — well, nothing bad, anyway. She was a bit of a daft old bat, the woman, scratching about in her purse for coins, peering into it as if she'd forgotten her glasses. She gave up trying for the right money when the checkout girl sighed, and pushed a crumpled five-pound note into her hand instead, then put her purse on the counter while she packed the things into her message-bag. There wasn't much — just biscuits and a sliced loaf and some fish fingers. The girl counted the change into her hand and off she went with it. I said, 'She's left her purse!' and the girl at the checkout shouted after her, but the old woman didn't hear. So I said, 'I'll catch her,' and grabbed the purse and went after the old woman and gave it back to her, and she seemed all puzzled and looked in her bag as if she was sure it must have been there all the time, then she said, 'Thanks, hen,' and shuffled off. But the thing was, in those moments of having someone else's purse in my hand, I had this sudden thought, what if it had hundreds of pounds in it, and belonged to someone stinking rich, not an old woman who lived on biscuits and bread and fish fingers? It was a horrible feeling, and yet so exciting.

But I wasn't in the supermarket. I was here in the classroom, and Angie was still writing furiously. 'Angie,' I said, 'listen.'

'Why?'

'I just thought. Do you remember the old woman in Tesco's who lost her purse?'

''Course I do. That's all part of it. Her and the alky. Isn't that what you meant?'

'Well, yes. But listen, I could have stolen her purse.'

'No, you couldn't, not with the checkout girl watching.'

'But what if it had fallen on the floor? I could easily have picked it up – and she didn't come back for it, she never knew it had gone.'

'You wouldn't have done, not to someone like that,' Angie said.

'*Fiction*,' I reminded her. Suddenly I was all excited about it. 'We could make her into someone else – a big man with a fat bum, yes, that's right, so his overstuffed wallet worked its way out when he pushed it back there after buying what he wanted.'

'Hey,' Angie said, putting her pen down, 'that's quite good. People would believe that. It's better than what really happened.'

'Shut *up*,' I said, and looked round nervously. What if someone had heard?

'Oh, sorry. That's great, though. What about the old drunk in the launderette? Are we keeping him?'

I hadn't got to him yet in my rememberings of that morning, but he seemed like an OK thing to use. 'Why not?' I said. 'He can go in at the beginning, because of me – I mean, Jez – not having enough money to give him. That could start her off, trying to get more.' Like it had started me? No, not really. With me, it had been a much older idea, and much more urgent. Not just the forest. Something that waited for the dark, so that it could haunt my dreams.

'Right,' said Angie, and picked up her pen again. I looked at the line-and-a-half I had written, and took a deep breath. I wrote, 'Jazz went off to get the *Motor Cycle News* for her brother, so Jez was sitting in front of the driers (dryers?)

on her own. A man came in, and he was drunk. He was asking all the people for money but they said no. Then he asked Jez, and she said yes, but she only gave him 10p because it was her mum's money, and he said he wanted more. A woman shouted at him and he went away.'

It was so embarrassing, the way he stood staring at the coin I'd given him, rocking a bit, and then looked at me with his eyes all red-rimmed and said, 'Ye couldny make it fifty, pet?' And I started trying to explain about my mum and the service wash, and he said, 'Ach, c'mon,' and it was then the woman next to me got up and shouted at him, 'Away ye go afore I get the polis.' And when he'd gone she started on at me about giving money to people like that because they'd only buy booze with it, and she was still bawling me out when Angie came back with the paper for Vikram and wanted to know what was going on.

'Yer wee friend,' the woman said, 'tryin' to give money to one of they alkies. He was all for gettin' more — you know the way they are.' And Angie said, 'She's no' been here long,' as if I was some sort of idiot. I said it was much worse in London, and they both looked at me as if to say, in that case I should have known better, and the woman got up and snatched

the dryer's door open and hauled out a blue nylon overall that crackled as she folded it up and rammed it into a plastic laundry bag.

That was the day Dad first met Vik. We went home on the bus with all these messages and the washing bags, and when we got there, Angie said, 'We're not heaving this lot up the stair. You stay and watch the stuff, and I'll bring someone down to help.' So she took a couple of the lighter bags and went off up to her flat, and I stood there looking at Motor Cycle News and wondering how they could tell one bike from another, and then Angie came back with Vikram. He's darker than her, and much taller, and amazingly good-looking. It was the first time I suddenly wished I was older. He laughed when he saw me reading his paper, and said he could see me on a Harley Davidson, then Angie's sister Sylvia came down as well, and she and Angie took the rest of the messages up to their flat, and Vik went bounding up our steps two at a time with the laundry bags and I followed with the things I'd bought for Mum.

Vik said he wouldn't stop because his mother had lunch ready, but Mrs Khan must have kept his hot for him for a long time that day, because he and Dad got talking about fitted kitchens. I knew Vik was at college, but I thought he was doing some kind of degree in English or Maths or something – it never occurred to *me that he might be doing something practical. But it turned out he was in Building Trades, specializing in cabinet-making, and that was right up Dad's street. I could see Vik was hoping Dad would give him a job for the summer, because it would be better experience than working in a pub like he was doing, but Dad said, the way things were, he hadn't enough work to keep himself occupied, let alone anyone else. But he'd put adverts all over the place, he said, and you never knew. At the moment it was mostly odd jobs, but if he landed a big one, he'd let Vik know.*

Before that conversation, I hadn't known much about what Dad was doing. I knew he'd sold the car and bought a van, and he kept looking through the paper for bankrupt sales where he could pick up cheap tools, but I hadn't really clocked that when a firm goes bust, it means you don't have any money. I can see now that he and Mum were trying to be really good parents and not let me feel insecure. They were always saying things like, 'It'll be all right,' and 'Don't you worry.' It was so nice of them – but I'd rather have known.

When Ian was there, it didn't matter so much if Mum and Dad didn't tell me things, because we had lots of laughs, even though he was so much older than I was. We'd pretend things, for days on end sometimes, like being the crew of a battleship, or a butler and housemaid in a Victorian house. I'd do little curtsies and say things like, 'Yes, m'm,' and he was very stiff and solemn, with a silver salver. We got it from some television programme. Or we'd be Japanese tourists, taking imaginary photographs of Mum and Dad and shrieking, 'Ah, so! Breeteesh family life!' Dad didn't take much notice, but Mum would say, 'Ian, when *are* you going to grow up?' And she'd glance from him to me and back again with a little shake of her head, as if to remind him that he shouldn't get me over-excited.

I must have seemed a lot better behaved after Ian left home, but I was dead miserable, really. If only Ian had kept his promise to write to me, it wouldn't have been so bad. He did at first, and I wrote back, but I wasn't much good at writing, not then. I drew silly pictures for him, but it's not the same as being together and having these mad ideas. So he didn't write as often, and it would be postcards instead of letters. They were funny postcards, but I knew they saved him from having to write so much. After a bit, he just put a few lines for me at the bottom of his letters to Mum.

These days, it's not even that. 'Love to Kelly,' he puts. Now that he's living with Susan, I suppose he's changed into a proper grown-up. I never thought he would.

Anyway, a day or two after the launderette episode, there was a phone call from a woman in Hyndland.

Granda took the call, because everyone else was out, and he said she sounded dead posh. She wanted her kitchen completely rebuilt, and she might want a conservatory, too. 'Conservatory,' Granda snorted. 'Turnin' us into the lap-dogs of capitalism, so y'are.' Nobody took any notice. Mum went out and bought Dad a new shirt 'for luck', and he put it on and went round to see the woman. He came back smiling all over his face. 'Ya beauty!' he said, rubbing his hands and sounding unusually Glasgow in his excitement. 'She's on for it. Just back from abroad, rich widow, bought this socking great house – even going to get a landscape firm to do the garden, and you know what they charge. She wants the kitchen built in from scratch, and with any luck I'll get the conservatory job as well, long as I can head her off from one of these specialist firms.'

Then, of course, there was the question of whether he was going to employ Vik. 'She wants the job done sooner than yesterday,' he said. 'She'll expect to see more men on it than just me.'

Mum was doubtful. She said it was important to keep the expenses down — maybe she was regretting being so rash about the shirt. But Dad said the job would be a good advert if they could do it quickly and well. 'You can see the woman's point,' he said. 'Nobody wants to live in a guddle of sawdust and plaster for days on end.'

'What's she move in for, then?' Granda demanded. 'Could she no' stay in a hotel or something? Or does she want to be on the spot so she can crack the whip over yez?'

'She's paying the bill,' Dad pointed out. 'And I'd only need Vik for a week or two, while we do the heavy stuff.'

Granda said, 'Oh, we're one of the bosses now, are we? Take a man on when ye need him, lay him off when it suits ye. Never thought I'd live to see the day.'

Dad looked at him and said, 'You're a political dinosaur, you know that?' And Granda said, 'Better than being a vampire,' and looked pleased with himself.

Mum sighed, and asked if someone would pass her the salad cream. She wasn't really into argument, not like the others. Granda loved it, though. Through a mouthful of pork pie, he said, 'Aye, the power o' the

bosses. Sittin' in judgement on the lives o' workin'
men.'

'And women,' I said, because I was getting the hang
of this political stuff now, and he nodded and said,
'Ye're right, pet.'

Dad said to me, 'Don't you start.' Then he turned
back to Granda. 'Look,' he said, 'the woman's bought
herself a house, so she wants to live in it. What's the
matter with that? She'll be wanting to settle down and
meet a few folk — she's just back from living abroad.
Her husband died out there.'

'Out where?' Granda asked.

Dad looked a bit uncomfortable. 'Well, South
Africa,' he admitted, 'but that's not to say—'

'South Africa!' Granda almost choked on his spring
onion. 'You do pick them, don't you?'

Dad gave up trying to be reasonable. 'Listen,
you daft old prat,' he said. 'Just because I do a job for
a woman whose husband used to work in South Africa,
it does not mean I am out there massacring Blacks in
the townships.'

And then they were at it ding-dong. Mum looked
resigned and went on eating, but I'd had a thought
which was so important and so awful that it made my
stomach lurch, and I couldn't touch another mouthful.
This woman was rich. And if Granda was right, it
sounded as if she might be really bossy and horrid, as

well. A sort of female Guy of Gisborne. She was the right and proper target for someone who wanted to keep faith with Robin of Lockesley, and with Andrew Carnegie, who thought that to die rich was to die disgraced. And with Granda, to whom I had made a promise, even if he didn't know it. He was arguing fiercely, with his white hair in wild untidiness and a knobbly fist clenched as he banged the table.

'Had enough, love?' Mum asked as she reached for my uncleared plate. She didn't fuss in those days about me leaving food. But then, it wasn't usual, not then. I used to eat lots.

I said, 'Yes, thank you,' but I wasn't really paying attention. I was wondering how Robin managed to be so brave. These words like justice and honour and kindness are all very well when you read them in books, but the thought of trying to put them into practice made me quake with fear.

Chapter 6

There I was, still in Miss Currie's English lesson. It's weird when you come back from a long spell of being somewhere else in your mind, you think hours of time must have gone past, but it hasn't. There was still the babble of noise, and Miss Currie going from table to table, encouraging people to do some work. She came to me and looked at what I'd written. I thought she'd complain about the spelling, or say it wasn't enough, but she just said, 'That's good, Kelly, keep trying.'

There was even less conversation between her and Angie.

'All right, Angela?'

'Yes, thank you.' And after a brief smile, Angie went on writing. She was the ideal pupil, really – nobody ever had to teach her at all.

I tried not to listen when it came to people reading out what they'd written. They were always slow and stumbly (not that I was any better), and you knew what sort of thing they'd have thought of anyway, so it was just boring. At least with Art nobody asked you to read out what you'd put down – the picture spoke for itself. I was praying Miss Currie wouldn't pick on me, and it was all right, she didn't. But she made an announcement which was even worse.

'I've some exciting news for you,' she said, looking like Father Christmas and the tooth fairy all rolled into one. 'Mr Jamie thinks our project is so worthwhile, he's been in touch with the local paper, and the editor has agreed to print the best novel that results from it. So you've a chance here to see your work in thousands of copies, being read all over this part of Glasgow. Isn't that great!'

Sharon and one or two others looked dutifully excited, but most of the boys groaned. Well, they had to, really. You can't have any street cred for writing a *story*, it's totally uncool. Angie looked at me and raised her eyebrows, but I was in a shrunken heap, wishing I was a snail that could get back into its shell. It was just the most horrendous thing I'd ever heard of. Angie was bound to win it, and my stupid Robin Hood act would be plastered all over the paper for Mum and Dad to read, and the Khans – *Vik*, for goodness' sake – not to mention the dreaded woman in Hyndland. The thought of it gave me the shudders.

I put my hand over my face and shut my eyes,

and Miss Currie asked if I was feeling all right. I said I'd got a bit of a headache. Well, I had to say something. But if I'd told her the real truth, I'd have said the whole wretched Project was an absolute pain in the bum.

Angie stayed on at school for her flute lesson that night, so I went home without her. Granda was in the kitchen on his own, as usual. Mum had just started this part-time job she's got at an estate agent's, and she never gets in until twenty to six.

'Hi, Kelly,' Granda said, 'How're ye doin'?'

I gave him his paper and said, 'All right.'

He knew it wasn't all right, of course. He always does. 'What's the matter, pet?' he asked. 'They givin' you a hard time?'

'Not really.' I was in such a muddle, I couldn't talk about it, even to him.

He said, 'OK.' Then he hobbled over to the sink and tipped the cold tea out of the teapot, together with its soggy teabags, which he scooped up and bunged in the bin. 'Is it one of the teachers?' he asked. 'You just tell me an' I'll bash his heid in.'

'You and whose army,' I said.

He swilled hot water in the pot, tipped that out, threw in a couple of teabags and poured on boiling water from the kettle. I watched him. 'It's not a teacher,' I said. 'It's English.'

'*English?*' He looked really concerned. 'Aw, c'mon, Kelly, English is a great subject.'

'Not the way we do it.'

'What ye doin', then? What ye readin'?'

'Nothing. We've to write this novel.'

Granda gave a hoot of laughter. 'Now, that is pure rubbish,' he said. 'Kids of your age – you'll excuse me, Kelly – but ye haveny lived. See, novels, they're – they're the distillation of human experience.' He nodded, pleased with the phrase. 'Now, if youse was to work wi' a writer, learnin' the craft of the thing, that would be something. Apprenticeship, like. But ye canny do it on yer own.'

'It's not just that,' I said, but he was off on one of his rants, and I'd have to wait until he'd said his piece.

'See, when ye're a kid, that's when ye've time to read. Scott, Dickens, Dostoevsky – they're the bedrock of the mind, Kelly. Start wi' the easier yins, if ye like – there's wee Graham Greene's no' a bad writer, and folk like George Orwell, and yer moderns – how about McIlvanney, now there's a man. But *read* – read an' understand. This stuff they're up to now, I tell ye, it's just constipation of the mind.'

He could always make me laugh, even if he had filched it from Rab C. Nesbitt on TV. 'Where's this tea, then?' I said.

He poured it out, and we sat there, munching Jaffa cakes (I could never resist a Jaffa cake, Thin Fund or no Thin Fund), and I rehearsed various ways of telling him about the Project and how awful it would be if it got in the paper, but each one seemed as difficult as the last. There had always been this unspoken agreement in the house that we would not mention what had happened last year. The disgrace of it was too embarrassing. In the end, he helped me.

'Ye were saying, Kelly, about this novel.'

Just tell him, I thought. It's only Granda. He's OK. 'See, when this writer came,' I said, 'Willa Pargett. She said we'd to dream up some fantastic story. It could be about spies or drug-smuggling or – or anything. Only the trick was, she said, to put it in a setting we knew, so's to do realistic descriptions, then people would believe it.'

'Canny argue wi' that,' Granda said. 'The woman knows what she's doing. So what's yer trouble?'

'Well, we thought – that is, Angie thought –

we could do a sort of Robin Hood story.' My face was flaming. 'Use what happened to me.'

Granda looked grave. 'Tha's no' exactly fantastic, is it, Kelly?'

'No, but Angie says, if we change it and change all the people, nobody will know it was me. And she says it'll sound just as fantastic as any other story about — well — crime.'

'Ye musny let Angie bully you, pet. I know she's a good pal, but—'

'She didn't. Didny.' I was getting my languages mixed. 'It was both of us. I know it was silly, but I couldny think of anything else.'

Granda thought about it, looking at me carefully. 'See,' he said. 'It might be a good thing. There's times ye need to look back at something tha's happened. What's to be the name of this story?'

'*The Sherwood Hero*,' I said, and blushed again. 'Angie thought of it.'

'Aye, tha's no' bad,' he said. 'An' it's you's the hero?'

'Yes. Only I wasn't, I know I wasn't. And the thing is, it's turned into a kind of competition. The best one's to get printed in the *Advertiser*. Everyone'll read it. And I'm sure Angie's and mine will get picked — she's so good.'

'Yer mother willny like that.'

'She'll be furious. I mean, there was nothing heroic about it.'

'I'm no' so sure,' Granda said. I stared at him, hopelessly confused. He ran his fingers through his white hair and frowned as he thought it over. 'See,' he said, 'ye shouldny put yerself down, pet. It was a brave thing ye did. Times have changed, an' we canny work things the way folk used to, but ye wereny to know that.'

I shook my head. There was this solid weight in the middle of me somewhere, a great lump of the awful feeling that had been left after those dreadful events, and that didn't melt away although it was all supposed to be forgotten. The bad dreams had started again, too, about the same things, the fires, the staring faces.

'When a bairn is born, it disny ken what century it's in,' Granda said. 'Ye get to understand that as ye grow up, an' start to see how things work round about ye. Some weans get wise to all that early on, see a lot of adult life – too much, sometimes. But your mum and dad have taken a lot of care of you, Kelly. When ye came up here, ye wereny a lassie that knew her way around – know what I mean?'

'Yes.' Angie had asked if I was an only child.

Compared with her, I'd been wrapped up in cotton wool. I couldn't blame Mum and Dad, though. If the baby before me had died, you could see they wanted to be extra careful.

'So there was you wi' a notion of how to set the world to rights, only ye tried to do it the same way as the outlaws tried, back in the Middle Ages,' Granda went on.

It was nice of him to make that excuse for me, but I'd never been quite that daft. Or had I? This was what puzzled me. There was something so scary about it, as if I'd had to do it for a dare, to prove I was on the right side, a goodie rather than a baddie. But I had ended up being bad, just because I had tried to be good. I'd have done better not to have tried at all. Could that be right?

Granda was puzzling over it as well, I could see that. 'It seems to me things are no' real these days,' he said. 'Not like when money was gold coins, or ye'd barter a sheep for four geese or something like that. See these computer hackers, they can slide a few figures into some programme –' he made a wriggling movement with his hand, like a fish – 'and there's them, rich. Same wi' doin' good. Ye put your name on the appeal form they send ye, credit-card number, ten quid, and away it goes, click-click-click through the computers, an' milk powder gets to some poor weans wi' bulgin' bellies in Africa. At least, ye hope it does. It's no' real. Just a big kid-on.'

He was as bad as me. Neither of us could work out why I'd got myself into all that mess last year. And I couldn't remind him of what he'd said in the café, that day when we went to the library, about taking the law into his own hands. Perhaps he hadn't meant it. I looked at him, trying to decide, and he seemed to know what I was thinking. 'Maybe I'm the one who's no' real, Kelly,' he said, gazing into his tea-mug as he swilled the dregs round and round. 'A dinosaur, like yer dad says.' And then he looked up, full of fight again. 'But I'll tell ye what. I'd sooner be a dinosaur wi' dreams of a better world than one of yer pin-striped men wi' a mind like one of they pocket calculators.'

We grinned at each other, then I picked up my school bag and said, 'I'd best get on with this homework,' and he said, 'that's it, Kelly, priorities,' and reached for the *Evening Times*.

What I really wanted to do was go on remembering. Granda had made me feel a bit braver, I suppose. For the first time, I felt an urge to unpack all those stuffed-away events, even though some of them were not going to be at all nice. I started on the Maths homework, but I'd only done a couple of questions before I found myself back at the beginning of that nightmarish day in the summer of the previous year.

CHAPTER 7

We'd only been living in Granda's flat for a few weeks, and the place was still upside down because Mum had said it had to be completely redecorated before she put our belongings into it. So everything reeked of paint, and most of our things were still waiting to be unpacked from their crates and boxes, and we ate and slept in a great clutter of paint pots and trestles and buckets – all except Granda, that is. He said his room was all right the way it was, thank you very much, and he'd have nobody interfering with it.

I woke early on that particular morning, even though there's nothing I like better than a long lie-in when I don't have to get up and go to school. I hadn't started at the Glasgow school, because it was still holiday time, though it didn't feel much like a holiday with all the decorating to be done. I lay and thought about the conversation over tea the previous day, when Dad had just come back with his news about the Hyndland job. I'd tried really hard to get myself taken on as a helper. 'I can paint,' I said. 'And I plastered a crack yesterday, and you said it was pretty good for a first go.' I was desperate to get into the woman's house, even though I was beginning to dread it. I didn't want to chicken out of my promise, you see. That's so easy, isn't it, saying you'll do something when you're all charged up about it being right, then changing your mind when it seems a bit tricky. Dad wasn't on for it, though, even when I pointed out that I wouldn't need to be paid. He laughed. Not that he meant it unkindly, he wasn't like that, but just because it was a silly idea.

'For what I'm charging this woman,' he said, 'she'll expect to employ proper tradesmen, Kelly. I'm taking a risk, even with Vikram, because she'll probably think he's just a boy. But I can't manage without him. I just hope he turns out to be as good as he sounds.'

There was nothing I could say. Granda was no help, either, because he got the wrong end of the stick about my efforts to help, and started muttering about child labour and exploitation. Mum said firmly that Dad would be taking Vik, not me, and I would not set foot in the place, but that didn't stop Granda. He just went off on a tirade about garage owners who employed what he called 'laddies who didny know one end of a spanner from the other' and paid them rubbish wages, while charging their work out at twenty pounds an hour. Dad said he had never exploited anyone, and he would pay Vik the right rate for the job. If Granda really wanted something to grumble at, he added, what about solicitors? They charged five times as much as garages, and most of their work was done by underpaid clerks. Mum shovelled chunks of Arctic Roll into bowls and said, 'Eat that before it thaws.'

'Aye, in some folks' hot air,' Granda said.

Anyway, perhaps I woke early because I was still wishing I was going off with Dad in the van. Crazy, really. What did I expect to find in the woman's house? Jewel caskets like the pictures in fairy-tale books, with ropes of pearls hanging out of them? Maybe I did, in a way. It's the gap again, between the way you imagine a thing and the way it really is. If you just say the word 'rich', it makes you think of people in wonderful clothes swanning into grand hotels, and taxis being whistled for by men in white gloves and top hats, and gilt trolleys piled with amazing food, and women dripping with diamonds. Perhaps I've watched too many old films on TV. I didn't really think the Hyndland house would be Aladdin's cave, but I wanted to get there all the same, so that I could relieve Mrs Moneybags of some of her surplus wealth and give it to people who really needed it.

Yes, I had been intending to steal, I can admit that now. I mean, I don't have much choice, do I? But at the time, I was still kidding myself I was doing a Heroic Deed.

I went on lying in bed, and heard the radio turned on in the kitchen, and dishes being put on the table, and the toaster popping up. Mum would be making Dad's sandwiches, packing them in his lunch box with a flask of coffee. I could hear their voices through the wall, though not what they were saying. I remember thinking it must be nice, having someone as close as that, to get up with in the morning and share everything. The Khans would be doing the same kind of things next door, chatting amiably and packing lunch boxes. Mr Khan always took his own food because he said he liked it better, and this morning there would be Vik as well. Lucky Vik.

A few minutes after Dad had gone, Mum tapped at my door. I pretended I was still asleep, but she didn't take any notice of that. She came in and said, if I was keen on helping to get houses to rights, there was plenty to be done here. She sounded a bit ratty, but she was right, of course. I'd helped a bit, off and on, but she'd been labouring away at the decorating every day since we moved in, and she was nowhere near finished yet. I said I'd be up in a minute.

I was pretty conscientious that morning. I spent hours up a ladder, washing the hall ceiling. It was a pale grey colour, all cobwebby, but when you rubbed it with a wet cloth, it turned darker, and water ran down your arm and bits of plaster fell in your hair. At about half past eleven, Angie came round and said, 'Hi. Having fun?' I said, 'Terrific,' and wrung the cloth out again, although the water in the bucket had turned to a gritty plaster soup.

Vik had forgotten his lunch box. Angie said he'd been so anxious not to oversleep he'd been awake half the night, and then when the alarm went off, he did oversleep. That's what he'd said, anyway, as he hurtled out of the house. All the others had thought he was up, because with so many people in and out of the bathroom, any one of them could have been him — and then they heard Dad hooting his horn in the street. Working in pubs gets you used to being up late and sleeping late, Angie explained as she stood there in our hall with Vik's lunch box. She was going to bike over with it, only she needed to know where the woman lived. And would I like to come.

That was when I got my first real attack of butterflies. I'd thought I'd been let off the hook and I wouldn't have to do it, then suddenly it was all on again. Angie knew what I wanted to do, because we'd had long talks about it after that first meeting at the funeral. She didn't know I planned to do it that very day, though, as we hadn't met since Dad came home with his good news, but she kept giving me funny looks, sort of challenging. She said afterwards, it seemed a good *opportunity, and she was interested to see if I meant what I said. That's Angie for you.*

Mum was horrified at the idea of me riding a bike in the Glasgow streets. I hadn't had a bike since I grew out of my little one in London, where I used to ride it down to the park and back with Dad on Saturdays, but Angie said I could borrow Sylvia's. The hallway of their flat was full of bikes. Mum still wasn't on for it, and I had to throw a real wobbler before she gave in. I went on about being bored and cooped up and treated like a baby and having no life, and I was so pent up about the idea of lifting money from some strange woman's house that it was pretty easy to get really upset.

Mum let me go, of course. She always used to be really nice to me then. She made me promise to get off the bike and walk it across zebra crossings, and she came down to see that it was the right size and that I could manage it properly. I wasn't at all sure that I could, I felt so shaky – I'd been to the toilet twice. Talk about butterflies, it felt more like a great snake churning about in my stomach. Angie got impatient and said she was going now, otherwise Vik wouldn't get his lunch in time for his lunch break, so off we went, with Mum calling last-minute instructions.

I sat there in the window seat, a whole year later,

remembering it all. One or two street lamps came on outside, although it was still light. They shone dull red at first, until they warmed up and turned orange. I heard Dad come in and start talking to Granda in the kitchen. Mum wasn't in yet. I ought to go and give a hand with peeling tatties or something, I thought – but I couldn't stop remembering, not now I'd started.

It was one of those big old houses with steps up to the front door, semi-detached. Dad's van was parked in front of it, and there were straggly bushes hanging over the wall, fuchsia with those little red dangly flowers, and that purple thing Mum calls the butterfly bush. The grass and nettles were knee-high, and you couldn't see where the path had been, just a track worn by people going round the side of the house. We took the bikes into the garden and parked them against the wall.

I hadn't thought it would be like this. The house was a big one, as Dad had said, very tall, with lots of sash windows and a flight of stone steps up to the front door, but it all looked so neglected and ordinary, I didn't even want to go in. There would be no ropes of pearls lying about. No jewel boxes. That dream had vanished. I was beginning to feel sure there would be no money, either. But Angie was getting Vik's lunch box off her bike carrier, and it was too late to wish I had never come.

The woman must have seen us from one of the front rooms, because suddenly there she was, at the front door. She came down the steps and said, 'Now, what have we here?' looking at me and Angie as if we'd been circus animals or something. Her face was very wrinkled, as if the skin was too tightly stretched, and her hair was a lemony white, in puffy curls. She wore a checked tweed skirt and a pink jersey with a string of pearls, and she was smoking a cigarette. Her fingers were yellow with nicotine.

'My brother forgot his lunch box,' Angie said, holding it up.

The woman glanced at the sky, implying that you couldn't expect anything else from people like us, and in that moment, I knew I loathed her. That made it worse. If she'd been nice, I could never have done it. But everything seemed to be nudging me on. 'Go round to the kitchen,' she said, with a wave of her cigarette. 'I'll see you there.' And she went back up the steps and into the house, shutting the front door behind her.

She was the stuck-up kind, I thought, as we made our way along the muddy path round the side of the house. She would have ridden through the greenwood on a white palfrey with those scalloped dangly things on the reins, and henchmen all round her, with spears.

Robin of Lockesley would have known her for what she was. But Robin was long gone, and there was nobody to defend the things he had fought for. Granda believed them, all right. 'If I wisny so old, I'd do it,' he'd said. But he was sitting in the flat, with his sticks propped against the table. There was only me.

When we arrived at the kitchen door, Dad was not pleased to see us. He frowned and said, 'I'm sorry, Mrs Melrose, I don't know what all this is about. Kelly, what are you doing here?' He probably thought I was still trying to get myself taken on as a kitchen-fitter's assistant. I couldn't blame him.

Mrs Melrose said, 'Don't worry, Mr Ferguson, I'm quite used to this sort of thing. Come along in, you girls, I expect you'd like some lemonade.' We went in, wiping our feet carefully although the kitchen was a total mess, with all the fittings ripped out, and a fridge with tea-making things on top of it standing like an island in a sea of sawdust and bits of timber. From the room next door, we could hear a sound of heavy hammering. Angie was explaining again about the lunch box, and the woman nodded in the direction of the hammering and said, 'Your brother's in the dining room, dear.' And when Angie had gone, she turned to Dad and remarked, 'That's the only trouble with them, Mr Ferguson. Once you get one, you do tend to get the whole tribe.'

Granda would have waded in straight away about racist remarks, but Dad shot me a glance of warning not to say anything. This job was important for him. The woman got a bottle of fizzy lemonade out of the fridge and offered me some, but I said, 'No, thank you.' I don't like fizzy drinks, but I'd have said no even if it had been fresh orange, honest I would.

She went on talking to Dad. 'I've so much experience of these people, you see,' she said. 'Of course, out in Africa one is absolutely dependent on them, I'm the first to admit that — but there are always these little drawbacks.'

I said, 'Angie's my best friend.'

'And very nice, too,' the woman said. 'I'd never encourage prejudice.' She had filled the kettle and was standing beside the fridge, putting mugs on a tray. 'Now you've stopped, Mr Ferguson, we'll call this the lunch break,' she said. And she looked at me and added, 'Go and call your friends, dear.'

I went through the kitchen door into the hall, where the light was dim and greenish because of the ivy growing across the front door. It was then that the real panic hit me. It was easy to dream about being the hero who did the great good thing, but this was real. If I meant it, I had to do it, this very morning. And my stomach churned. Vik was still hammering in one of the rooms behind me, to the left of the kitchen. The doors of the front rooms stood ajar. What if there was someone sitting in one of them, aware of me out here in the hall, listening for my next move?

I had to tell Angie and Vik to come for their tea, I thought, so I couldn't do it right now, the woman would be expecting us back in the kitchen. But I could at least look in the rooms. I clenched my sweaty hands. I will do it, I promised Granda and Robin and Andrew Carnegie and all the unknown people who were on the side of justice, I will. I'm not a coward.

Oh, but I was. Thinking about it as I sat curled on the window seat, I remembered the crawling terror that seemed to turn my guts to water, and how I tiptoed forward to stare in through the door on the left, then the one on the right.

Nobody sat waiting in either of them. The one on the left was still unfurnished, with a lot of tea chests in it, and chairs up-ended on top of other chairs, and shapeless things under dust sheets. But the other one had been newly decorated. It had pale green textured wallpaper and a flowered carpet, and there were chintzy sofas and several little upright chairs with curvy legs, and I caught sight of myself in gilt-framed mirror over the fireplace, looking weirdly ordinary. But in the next minute, I had forgotten about everything else, because there was a handbag on the seat of the armchair by the fire. A black handbag, open, with an upside-down magazine beside it, and a pair of glasses.

Oh, why did it have to be there? But I knew why. When you are meant to do something, it's no use resisting. Everything will invite you to it. I just looked at the bag, then fled towards the sound of hammering in the back room, barging in through that door as if I was chased by ghosts. Angie looked up, and went all bright with interest when she saw me. I was probably looking frantic. But I just said, 'She wants you in the kitchen for tea.'

Vik said, 'Great, I'm starving,' and Angie told him he'd have been more starving without his lunch box, and we went back into the kitchen. Mrs Melrose offered Angie some lemonade, and Angie said happily, 'Yes, please.'

Dad gave me another glance, even more meaningful this time, and I knew that when Angie had finished her drink, we were to take ourselves off. If I was going to do it, this was the last chance. I was in a cold sweat all over. I needed an excuse to get out of the room. I said, 'Please can I go to the toilet?' I thought everyone would notice that my voice didn't sound like me. But Mrs Melrose just said, 'It's next to the dining room –

where you've just come from. If you wash your hands, use soap, don't just wipe the dirt off on the towel.'

I remember not being able to look at Dad or Angie, and how I fumbled with the handle as I let myself out of the kitchen. Now. It had to be now. The handbag on the armchair.

There was no money. Just this note case with credit cards in it and a folded slip of paper. Angie was right. She'd said rich people paid for everything with cards. Fingerprints, I'd thought frantically, oh God, oh God. I pushed one of the cards and the scrap of paper into my jeans pocket, rubbed the note case on my T-shirt and dropped it back where it had been, then fled. The next thing I knew, I was being sick into the rose-pink lavatory bowl.

It caused a bit of a sensation when I went back into the kitchen. Dad said, 'Hey, Kelly, are you all right?' And Mrs Melrose raised her eyebrows and said she hoped I hadn't made a mess. I told her I hadn't, and it was true. I'd just got the lid of the toilet up in time. My fingers could still feel the soft thickness of its pink candlewick cover.

Vik said through a mouthful of sandwich, 'You look terrible.'

And Angie didn't say anything.

CHAPTER 8

It's funny how your body can behave as if it's somewhere else. There I was, perfectly safe, sitting on the window seat with the whole thing over and done with more than a year ago, and yet feeling as sick and clammy as if I was in Mrs Melrose's sitting room all over again, with my head pounding and my hands shaking.

Mum's key scratched in the lock, and I was glad, because I knew she would call me to help set the table or something, and I'd be rescued from sitting here in a cold sweat. Sure enough, I heard her voice from the kitchen. 'Kelly – what are you doing?'

'Homework,' I called back. 'Just coming.' I uncurled my legs and stood up, feeling cramped, and went into the kitchen.

We had beefburgers for tea, and peas and chips, but I ate even less than usual. I was terrified Granda might mention what I'd told him about the Project, but it was OK – he didn't. He was great, he never even gave me a meaningful look. He and Dad were discussing something the

French president had done, and whether Europe was a good thing, and Mum was reading a magazine while she ate. But, of course, that left me free to think about other things. Tomorrow morning, Angie would be on about our story again. She'd want to know what we were to put after the fat man had dropped his wallet. What would Jez-the-hero do with the money? Angie didn't know much about what I'd done — it had been too awful to talk about.

Mum looked up from her magazine and said, 'You're very quiet tonight. What are you thinking about?'

I felt my face flame. 'Just school,' I said.

'What about it?' She was frowning.

Granda said quickly, 'Ach, it's just some lad sweet on her — that right, Kelly?'

I was so grateful to him, I probably looked suitably embarrassed, but Mum wasn't happy about that, either. 'For goodness's sake,' she said, 'you've no time to waste on *boys*, Kelly, you need to be concentrating on your schoolwork.'

She had a point, I suppose. My reports at this school had been dreadful, and I'd been quite good at the Primary in London. But then, they hadn't been so fussed about Maths and English and getting the answers right. I couldn't help it — I just never seemed to get interested. It wasn't just school, it was everything. I felt sort of vague and detached. Nothing seemed to matter. I didn't *want* it to matter. I only wanted to be undisturbed, not to have to think. It had been awful since that writer came, with Angie nagging at me all the time. My brain positively ached.

There was chocolate mousse for pudding, but I said I didn't want any. Mum sighed. I muttered something about finishing my homework, and went back to my room.

I'd have to be firm with Angie, I thought. I wasn't going to be pushed into all this uncomfortable remembering. Right now, I was not going to think about it for one more minute.

The Maths homework seemed to have been going on for hours, because I'd started it when I came home from school, then got sidetracked by the dreadful rememberings. Maths is so boring, anyway. It's not *about* anything, only itself. And it's so bossy, making you into a slave to its finicky little rules. But I wrote down some sort of answers and shut the jotter, then went and watched TV with everyone else.

Other people watch TV quietly, but not the Fergusons. We argue about it. Mum said there was nothing worth watching now that *Cheers* had finished, and Granda snorted and said it was a load of American rubbish. Dad couldn't resist stirring him up. 'If you ask me,' he said, 'America is the only country in the world that's truly progressive.'

'Aye, they progress like a drunk man wi' a paper bag over his head,' Granda told him. 'See that Columbus – Ah tell ye, we'd a been better off if he'd sunk in mid-Atlantic.'

They were at it hammer and tongs after that. Even Mum joined in, and you couldn't hear anything the telly was saying. I watched the faces on the screen for a bit, and concentrated hard on not thinking.

It was all waiting for me when I went to bed, though. I shut my eyes and tried to go to sleep, but there I was, standing in Mrs Melrose's front garden with Angie, and the taste of having been sick still in my throat, sharp and sour. The credit card and the slip of paper were in my jeans pocket, and my legs were shaking.

Angie said, 'You did it, didn't you.'

I nodded. Couldn't speak.

'What was it? Cash? Credit card? No, that would be no use.'

'Yes,' I managed to say. 'Credit card.'

She was cross. 'Honestly, Kel, you're such a bampot. Cards are no good without the number. I mean, if you're going to do it, you might as well do it properly.'

I said, 'There's a bit of paper.' I wanted to get away from the house. The woman might be watching us through the window. She might be looking in her handbag. At any minute, she was going to phone the police, then come out of the front door and order us back into the house.

Dad came round from the kitchen, looking worried. He wanted to take me home in the van, but Angie said, 'She's all right, aren't you, Kel? We'll just go as far as the park and sit down for a bit. If she's still feeling rubbishy, I'll come back and get you, OK?' And she gave him her capable smile.

Dad was in what they call an agony of indecision, you could see that. He wanted to take me home, but he knew Mrs Melrose would be glancing at her watch, counting up pennies per second – and he really needed that job. 'Well, if you're sure,' he said. And after we'd done a lot of promising and reassuring, he went back to the kitchen, and we got on the bikes and escaped. We went down towards Partick, and stopped at what Angie had called the park. It was more of a playground, really. We sat down on a low wall on the edge of a kids' sandpit. Angie said, 'Let's have a look.'

She unfolded the slip of paper. It fluttered a bit in the wind. The sun had gone in behind clouds, and it was threatening rain. Then Angie laughed. 'Have you seen this?' she said.

I shook my head. There were things written on it, that's all I knew. In that sitting room, I hadn't been able to see anything properly, only the handbag, like an open crocodile's mouth.

'Talk about brilliant,' Angie said. She passed me the slip. I didn't want to look. It's like when you've cut your finger and you don't want to see what you've done. But when I saw what the paper said, I nearly laughed. It was gibberish, a mixture of words which meant nothing. The relief was wonderful. I was let off the hook, I couldn't use the card, I could put it in a bin somewhere and pretend the whole thing had never happened. The woman would think she'd lost it.

Lying in my bed, trying not to remember, I could see the small capital letters as clearly as I did on that cool summer afternoon.

AE WORM ANT MAN TRIPLE STOOL
V HORSE SCARECROW MAN MAN
A STOOL SPIDER HORSE SPIDER

Angie said, 'It must be a code.' She was frowning over it like she does over schoolwork, and my heart sank. She was determined to understand it. 'What card have you got?' she asked.

I passed it to her, and she looked at it and said, 'Visa. And were there others?'

'Yes.'

'What sort?'

'I don't know, I didn't look.'

Angie said, 'You're hopeless, Kelly, you know that? Call yourself a hero — you'd never get round to killing a dragon or anything, you'd get to its cave with your sword and decide dragons are nice wee things after all.'

'Dragons are all right,' I said. But Mrs Melrose wasn't all right. 'That woman, though — she called you and Vik a tribe.'

'Well, so we are,' said Angie, not a bit offended. She was still puzzling over the slip of paper. 'You can see what the first letters mean,' she said. 'V is for Visa, AE is American Express and A is Access. She must be off her head, fancy making it that obvious.'

I know now that people do it all the time, put their numbers down in code because they think they'll forget them, the police said so. But I didn't know it then.

'Come on, Kel,' Angie said, 'you ought to be helping.'

I said, perhaps it was the number of letters in the word or something, but Angie had already dismissed that. 'HORSE is the same number as STOOL,' she said. And she couldn't see why one of them had an extra word. 'Don't they all have four digits? I know my Dad's Visa card has. But the AE one's got five. Worm, ant, man, triple, stool.'

And that's where I blundered right into the trap. Hearing her read the words out made it easy to see them in a different way.

'Triple-stool,' I said, 'three of them, perhaps.' And I gazed in imagination at three nursery-rhyme milk-maids, seated by three brown cows, each maid on a three-legged stool. And then it hit me. 'Nine,' I said.

'Huh?'

'The number of legs. Stools have three. We had a table that wobbled, and Dad was always fiddling with it, trying to get it to stand level, and he said three-legged stools always do. Stand level, I mean. That's why they're good in cow sheds with rough floors.'

Angie said, 'You're joking.' Then she looked at the paper again and said, 'No, you're right. Horse, four legs, spider eight, man two. What about worm? Oh, none, of course.' She hit the side of her head for being stupid. 'Zero.'

'And scarecrow's one,' I said.

That threw Angie for a moment, and I had to explain how a scarecrow was built on a broomstick. It was funny how she didn't seem to see it like I did, with its hat and its straw hair, and the sleeves of its old coat stuck straight out sideways on the cross-piece. She shrugged and said, 'There you go, then. All yours.' And she pushed the card and the strip of paper back at me.

I don't know what she'd have said if I'd chickened out. Maybe she wouldn't have minded. She wasn't exactly keen on it, but she looked sort of fascinated, as if I'd been a conjuror, and she'd wanted to see what I'd do next.

Lying in bed all hot and restless, I rolled over for the umpteenth time on to my other side. I seemed to have been awake for hours. I'd heard Mum and Dad go to bed – Granda always stayed up later, reading. I seriously wanted to stop thinking about what had happened. We weren't going to use any of this credit-card business for the Project, anyway, that was for sure, so there was no point in replaying this mental video. Why couldn't I go to sleep? But the more I tried to forget it, the more I was back there in the playground, sitting on that low brick wall which edged the sandpit. Some little kid had lost a sock, a wee blue one. It lay there all dirty, soaked with last night's rain.

Angie warned me that, if anyone asked her, she wasn't going to know anything about it. That's when she pointed out that she couldn't risk getting a criminal record, not if she was aiming to be the prime minister. It made me feel very immature. But at the same time, I thought, at least I'm doing something practical about it, not just theorizing. She came with me to the cash dispenser, though, which was nice of her. It was the one in the entrance to Tesco's, where we'd gone on the day of the drunk in the launderette. It seemed a bit less frightening than a bank one. But I was terrified, all the same. I thought the row of red letters in the slot would say, THIS IS NOT YOUR CARD. But they didn't. When I put the card in, they said KEY PERSONAL NUMBER, as if I was a perfectly proper customer.

HORSE, 4, SCARECROW, 1, MAN, 2, MAN, 2.

KEY SERVICE REQUIRED.

And, of the list printed on the screen, I had selected WITHDRAW CASH. And then pressed the button by the arrow which pointed at £100.

If that was correct, the machine said in its friendly way, I should press PROCEED. And I pressed it.

That was the moment, wasn't it. The real crime. Until then, I could have backed out. But now, I'd done it. The notes offered their edges to me from their slot, and I took them. There were only six of them. Somehow, I had expected a huge handful.

Angie was waiting outside the automatic sliding doors, with both bikes. She didn't ask me if I'd managed it all right. She didn't say anything. We rode home and hauled the bikes upstairs to her flat, and it was only then that she said, 'OK?' and I said, 'Yes.'

Our flat was full of the smell of fresh paint, because Mum had finished scrubbing the hall ceiling while I'd been out, and had given it a coat of emulsion. I had to tell her I'd been sick at Mrs Melrose's house, because I thought Dad might have rung up to see if I was all right. But he hadn't. Mum said I'd probably got chilled riding that bike, and she had known it was a mistake letting me go. I didn't want to stand there talking to her, I wanted to get rid of the card and the money and the slip of paper, folded together in my jeans pocket. As soon as I could, I went and buried them deep under my winter woollies in the bottom drawer of the chest of drawers. Later that evening, I sneaked a pair of scissors and cut the card into small pieces.

CHAPTER 9

You feel really grotty in the morning if you've been awake half the night. I'd hardly slept, and I crawled on to the bus like the living dead, but Angie didn't seem to notice. She asked the question I was waiting for.

'What happens after the fat guy drops his wallet in Tesco's?'

'Don't know.'

'Yes, you do, Kel, come on. We're into the next chapter now, we've to do the bit about Feeding the Poor. We can put in that it was really difficult, can't we? Like you said.'

'I didn't say.'

'No. You didn't, did you. But it was pretty obvious. I don't know why you clammed up about it. I mean, I helped you crack the code. You'd never have bothered on your own.'

I looked round nervously in case anyone was listening, but there was nobody near us except a boy with rock music hissing loudly out of his headphones, and he wouldn't have heard anything.

But she hadn't wanted to be involved, because of her precious record. I felt too tired and cross to be polite. 'If you'd wanted to know what happened, you could have stayed with me, that morning when we went to Argyle Street,' I said. 'You just shoved off and left me to get on with it.'

'But I told you—'

'Yes, I know. Criminal record. So what are you moaning about? You didn't want to know, and I didn't tell you.' I wasn't being quite fair. 'In any case,' I added, 'it was – not a lot of fun. I didn't *want* to talk about it.'

'I could see that,' said Angie. 'You've looked as sick as a parrot ever since. You've got thin, too. My mum says it's not healthy.'

Your mum, I thought, can just mind her own business. But I didn't say it.

'Come on, Kel,' Angie said, trying to coax me. 'We haven't got much time. I was with you when you did the hole in the wall, right? That was on the Friday, just after we'd taken Vik his lunch box. How much money did you get?'

'A hundred pounds,' I said unwillingly.

'Is that all? I'd have gone for more. But it was big notes, wasn't it? You said you'd have to get change. Did you do that?'

I sighed. OK, I thought, you win. 'Yes, I did.

Mum made a fuss about me going out, of course, because I'd had to tell her about being sick at Mrs Melrose's, and she wanted me to stay in the warm. I said I had to get some fresh air. Angie, you're not to write this down.'

'I'm not,' Angie said. 'Look, I only put "Getting change".' She showed me her jotter.

'Oh, all right. Anyway, I couldn't go to the local shops in case they knew me. And I didn't dare go into a bank, I felt as if they'd have Wanted posters on the wall.'

'So where did you go?'

'I went right down to Dumbarton Road, and changed a twenty into two tens in a paper shop. I didn't dare change more than one, because they'd think it was funny. And the next shop wouldn't give me change if I didn't buy anything, so I bought an apple.'

'Just one? For twenty pounds?'

'Yes. It was a shop like your uncle's, with baskets of fruit and things outside.'

'I bet he wasn't very pleased.'

'Not very, no.'

'Then what?'

'Well, I had this problem about the apple. I mean, it wasn't mine, or I'd have been stealing for me, do you see?'

Angie nodded and said, 'Couldn't you give it away?'

'That's what I thought. There was this woman with a little kid, and she was wearing a coat that looked a bit Oxfam, so I offered the apple to the little boy, and he was going to take it, but she pulled him away and said, "No, *thank* you," and looked at me daggers.'

Angie giggled. 'You're such a twit,' she said. 'Who *did* you give it to, then?'

'Well—' I knew I was going to laugh, but it hadn't been funny at the time. 'I saw a bag-lady. You know, with broken old shoes and all her stuff in a supermarket trolley. And rat-nesty hair.'

'Well, she was poor, right enough,' Angie said.

'Yes, she was. And she smelt simply awful. I said, "Would you like an apple?" and she looked at it, then said, "Got no teef." And she hadn't. She couldn't eat it.'

Angie laughed so much I thought she was going to fall off her seat. I did, too, even though it had been so horrendous.

'What did you do with it in the end?' Angie asked when she'd recovered.

'I put it in a baby's buggy that was parked outside the Post Office. Only it might have belonged to someone quite rich. But how can you find out?'

'You can't, not without making people feel awful.' And Angie started on about her scheme for giving everyone an allowance. I wasn't listening, though, so she stopped talking about that, and asked what else I'd done. Nothing, I told her, because I'd been out for quite a while and I knew Mum would be getting agitated. And I'd only changed two twenties, and the coins and smaller notes made the whole pocketful feel bigger and heavier. Mum caught me on the way in, of course, and said how worried she'd been, and I stood there with this great bulging pocketful, certain that she'd notice it at any minute. I was relieved that nothing had happened, though. I'd been quite scared to come back in case there was a police car outside.

Angie listened to all that, and didn't write anything down, then she said, 'So that was it until the next morning – that Saturday when we went into town?'

I nodded. And then I knew there was something I had to ask her. 'Angie, when you came to call for me that morning, was it true you were going to buy a birthday present for Sylvia, and that's why you were going to Argyle Street? Or were you — being helpful?'

For once, Angie looked a bit embarrassed. 'Well,' she said, 'you'd have found it difficult on your own. You didn't know Glasgow — you'd only just come here.' Then she added, 'But it *was* Sylvia's birthday. Does it matter?'

Yes, somehow it did. All this time, I'd thought the Robin Hood affair had nothing to do with anyone else. That's what made it so awful, being completely alone in it. And now she was saying I needn't have been. 'You *were* involved, then,' I said.

Angie shrugged that off, pointing out that it didn't matter if she was involved or not, because we were only concerned with getting a story out of it for the Project. Perhaps it was silly of me to fuss, I thought, now the whole thing was over — but I felt irritated with Angie. Perhaps it was because I was so tired. I'd probably have gone to sleep on the bus if she hadn't been talking all the time.

'What *did* you do, anyway, that morning in Argyle Street?' she demanded. 'You might as well tell me.'

'There isn't time,' I said. 'We're nearly at

school. I'll write it all down in English.' Or some of it, anyway.

'And what am I going to do?'

I said rather bitchily that she'd just have to use her imagination.

Miss Currie's lesson was after morning break. I was feeling a bit better by then, but not much. I'd decided to do the Giving Away Money bit in the form of a list, just saying who got what. I wrote with my arm circled round my jotter like little kids do, so that Angie couldn't see. I didn't want her asking for details in the classroom with everyone listening. I started my list with *Man outside St Enoch's, £5.*

He was asking people for the price of a cup of tea, and when I gave him the fiver, he looked at it and then at me as if he thought I'd made a mistake. With Scotland still having one-pound notes, he might have thought I didn't mean to give him so much. He didn't say thanks or anything, just shoved the note into his pocket and hurried away.

Buskers, lots of coins. I hadn't counted how many.

The buskers had been all right, partly because you didn't have to put money into their hands, just drop it into a music case. But I wasn't going to write about how it had been. Just the list. *Boy with dog, £20.*

He was sitting on the pavement in that pedestrian bit of Gordon Street outside the travel agents', where there are trees in circular beds with low brick walls round them. They were both very thin, him and his dog, and he had a notice propped up that said Hungry and Homeless. But he argued about the money. 'I canny take all that,' he said. He wanted to know where I'd got it from. I'd already tried to give the same note to a man in Buchanan Street who was asking people for small change, but he'd said flatly, 'I'm no' takin' money from weans.' And the boy with a dog didn't want to take it, either. In the end I just walked off quickly and left him holding it. For the rest of the morning, I had to be careful not to go back along that street in case he was still looking for me.

I wrote down, *Hungry and Homeless*, for the sake of something to do while I thought about what happened next, and Miss Currie came by and said, 'That's very good, Kelly, well done.' She might not have thought it was good if she'd known what I'd really done. It was very embarrassing, going up to complete strangers and trying to give them money. One man said, 'Aw, get home to yir mother,' and spat on the pavement. And sometimes I simply got it wrong.

There was a woman in a duffle coat standing outside a bookshop looking sort of old and untidy, with grey hair, so I went up and held out a ten-pound note and said, 'I'd like to give you this' – and she was furious. She said, 'I beg your pardon!' in a dead snooty voice, and a man in a deer-stalker hat came out of the bookshop and said, 'What's the matter, Dorothy?' I didn't stay for any more, I just fled.

I tried to give the tenner to a man who was leaning against a wall. I could see he was drunk, but he had a smile on his face and I thought he was all right. He looked at the note I was offering him, then looked at me, and said, 'Now, why would you think I want that?' He had white bristly hair all over his chin and not many teeth, and he sounded Irish. 'Money brings happiness,' he said, waving his hand as if he was an actor on a stage. 'That's what they say. Isn't that right, darlin'?' I didn't know. 'Well, if it's not right,' he went on, 'then there's no use you tryin' to give me that, now is there? Because it wouldn't make me happy. An' if it is right, then ye're too late, because I'm happy already. So you'd best take yerself off, dear, because if ye're still here when my happiness has gone, I might be tempted to take yer cash, an' that wouldn't be right.' I said, no, it really was all right, and still tried to give it to him, and he stopped smiling. It was a bit frightening, really. 'Get off home,' he said, 'ye wee idjit. Put your money in your piggy-bank. One of these days ye might need it.'

I thought of him afterwards sometimes, when I was putting a fifty pence saved from my dinner money into my pink plastic piggy-bank. He knew more than I did.

And then there was the woman with a baby. I wouldn't have thought she was poor, because she looked quite ordinary, wearing a red jacket, tracksuit bottoms and trainers, and carrying the baby in one of those sling things — only I heard her asking a man with a briefcase if he could give her the train fare to Aberdeen. She started explaining how she needed to get there because she'd nowhere to live, and she wanted to stay with her sister, but the man just said, 'Sorry,' and went on. She asked a couple more people, with no luck, so I went up to her and said, 'How much is it to Aberdeen?' She said it was twenty pounds, and I gave it to her, but a woman who looked a bit like my mother saw what I did, and tried to interfere. She said it wasn't as much as that to Aberdeen, and the girl didn't want it for the train fare at all, she was going to buy drugs with it. The girl swore at her and ran off down the street with the baby jigging up and down in its sling, and the woman started on at me, wanting to know where my parents were and how I got the money and whether they knew, and I ducked away from her and nearly got hit by a taxi as I bolted across the road.

I wrote down, *Woman with Baby, £20.* There'd been a lot of walking about in between these meetings with people, because it's quite hard to find the Poor when you're looking for them, even though you know they're everywhere. Lots of times, I'd stop and look at someone, but after approaching the snooty woman who was so furious, I was scared of offending people. There must have been quite a few who really needed the money, and I didn't give them any because I was too much of a coward. But it's too late to think about that.

The best one was the boy selling The Big Issue. *'Magazine produced by the homeless!' he was shouting, just outside British Home Stores. 'Sixty per cent of the price goes to the vendor.' I gave him a ten-pound note and said I didn't want a magazine, and added quickly that the money was from my mum. I waved a hand to indicate that she was around somewhere, in one of the shops. I thought that was dead clever of me, but even so, there was a bit of an argument. The boy said, 'We're not allowed to take money as a gift, only to sell the magazine.' I didn't know what to say about that, but he gave me a sort of wink, counted out a few copies and pushed them into my hand. I don't think there were enough for ten pounds. 'Tell your mother, thanks a lot,' he said.*

The Big Issue, ten pounds. I'd forgotten about putting my arm round what I was writing, and Angie leaned across and saw it. 'Hey, that's a good idea,' she said. 'They're great, the *Big Issue* lot. My dad says it's a really well-organized business.'

'Business? But I thought—'

'All charity's a business, isn't it,' Angie said. 'I mean, someone's got to get the money from the public, and make sure it goes to the people who need it.'

She was so superior sometimes, it really annoyed me. And it wasn't true, anyway, not when you did something on your own. *I* hadn't been a business. But then, of course, a nasty little suspicion made itself felt. Maybe I'd made such a mess of it *because* I wasn't a business. I'd thought it would be easy to give money away, but it isn't, it's hellish. The *Big Issue* boy was much easier than the others because he offered you a proper deal, and you knew where you were. The buskers weren't too bad, either, with their instrument cases and their bits of cardboard with Thank You written on them – but the others were just scary. You didn't know what they'd say or do. That's why I'd been reduced to Oxfam in the end. It wasn't what I'd intended. Robin Hood didn't give to Oxfam. But then, he was a hero, and I wasn't, not by the time I'd finished, anyway.

Finished. Yes, it was that last man who had finished me. Even now, I felt queasy when I thought of him.

He was another drunk, standing at the Low Level entrance to Central Station, where it's rather dark under the railway bridge. He was wearing a greasy grey coat with a bit of string tied round it, and his eyes were shut, but he had his hand stuck out in an automatic sort of way, and I thought it would be reasonably easy to put some money into it. There would be no need to say anything, I'd just give him a ten-pound note and walk on. I had the note folded and ready. But at the touch of it on his palm he seemed to wake up with a start and he lurched, and the ten-pound note was caught in the draught that came blowing at that moment from the Low Level station. A train must have just come in. Anyway, we both grabbed at the tenner and missed it, and it fluttered down on to the pavement. I was scared it would blow away, so I stooped to pick it up – and the man was on top of me. I don't know if he lost his balance or what, but I was down on my knees under his weight, and the smell of him was sickeningly awful, and in the next minute he was clutching at me and muttering, 'Ye're lovely, pet, ye're lovely.' My hands were clawing at the pavement. I tore myself free and ran. Somebody said, 'Are you all right?' but I didn't stop. I ran and ran, across Union Street and along Argyle Street, past the bit where the buses turn in to the St Enoch Centre, along the pedestrianized bit with Marks & Spencer and Menzies. A man in a kilt was playing the bagpipes. I slowed down then, gasping for breath. I could still feel the clutching hands

*and the roughness of the dirty coat, and the foul smell
was still in my nose and my lungs.*

You're in the classroom, I told myself, you're all right. But my heart was pounding and my fists were clenched. Miss Currie smiled at me and said, 'Run out of ideas?' I shook my head.

I'd said I'd meet Angie at Central Station at twelve o'clock, and it was nearly five to. There was still some money in my pocket but I couldn't face any more, not after that man. I went up Queen Street because I didn't want to go back the way I'd come — I mean, what if he'd been looking for me? — and then had to avoid Gordon Street because of the boy with the dog, so I came to the station by a long way round. That's how I saw the Oxfam shop. I went in and rammed all the rest of the money into the collecting box on the counter. Nobody noticed because the woman was talking to her helper. 'I don't know how people manage without a mobile phone,' she was saying.

I was a bit late meeting Angie. She was standing outside the Sock Shop. 'OK?' she said, looking normal and cheerful, the way she does. I nodded and said, 'OK.' She'd bought a cassette for her sister's birthday, and started telling me all about what music Sylvia liked, and what Vikram and Moti and the others liked, and I felt as if I'd been dreaming. I walked with her to the bus. When it came, I realized I'd mixed my own money up with the remains of the Robin Hood fund, and put the whole lot in the Oxfam box. Angie looked at me pityingly and said, 'Honestly, you are a twit,' and lent me the money for the fare. My knees were bruised, and I ached all over. About halfway home, she asked me if it had been awful, and I said, 'Yes.' She gave me a bit of chewing gum, and I began to feel a bit better. I've liked chewing gum ever since. Angie didn't ask any more. She can be really nice sometimes.

When I got home, things were still all right. Granda said, 'Did ye no' buy yersel' a wee something, Kelly?' and I shook my head. I'd even dropped all the copies of The Big Issue. They'd be lying scattered on the pavement outside the Low Level station, under the bridge. The man probably found his tenner. I didn't much care. Mum said consolingly, 'There's no point in spending money just for the sake of spending it.' She still approved of me then.

I knew when Dad came in that it had happened. There was something about the way he closed the door behind him. When he came into the kitchen, he tossed his keys on the table and said, 'That's the last time I *take on a helper.'*

Mum said, 'Why? Has Vik made a botch of it?'

'Vik's done worse than that,' Dad said grimly. 'It looks as if he's pinched the woman's credit card.'

Mum gasped and said, 'Oh, no!' And Dad said, 'Oh, yes.' They stared at each other. Mum was absolutely horrified. 'I can't believe Vik would do a thing like that,' she said. 'They're such a nice family. Did Mrs Melrose get the police?'

'Did she,' Dad said. 'I tell you, we've been through the third degree this morning. Down to the station for questioning, who'd been in the house and when, how long I'd known Vik, whether I could vouch for his good character. What could I say? I only met the boy ten days ago. Made me look a right prat, I can tell you.'

Mum said, 'That's awful.' Granda was shaking his head, looking worried. I felt sick. I knew I would have to tell them I'd done it. I never thought the blame would fall on Vik. Let alone Dad. I said huskily, 'Dad—' But he said, 'Just leave this to us, Kelly.' And Mum said, 'Yes, it's nothing for you to worry about.'

Granda said, 'Maybe the woman just lost it.'

'No, she's quite positive it was in her wallet,' Dad said. 'She remembered having it to order something by phone, from a catalogue. She found it was missing this morning, when she went to get petrol for her car.'

'Ye can spend an awfu' lot on they wishin'-books,' Granda said, but they weren't going to be sidetracked. Mum was asking practical questions about where the card was kept, and as if I was in a dream, I listened to Dad telling her about the handbag and the wallet, and how only the Visa card had been taken, together with the strip of paper with the coded numbers on it. 'Whoever took it didn't waste any time,' he said. 'A hundred pounds went out of her account yesterday, and goodness knows what else they've had. Vik denies it, of course.'

'Ach, she must have dropped it,' Granda said. 'Did they check for fingerprints?'

'Yes, she insisted on that. Very smudged, they said, as if someone had wiped the wallet or held it wrapped in something. They couldn't prove it was me or Vik. Or that it wasn't.' He held out his still-grey fingertips, and Mum gasped again. Granda said, 'Pete's sake, how did the stupid woman leave her number with the card? There's posters everywhere tellin' ye to keep them separate.'

'She used some sort of code,' Dad said. 'A lot of people do, the police said, but it never works. She's cancelled the order for the conservatory, of course.'

Mum said, 'Oh, no.'

I had to tell them. I said in a dry croak, 'I did it.' But nobody heard me because they were all talking. I tried again, louder. 'I DID IT.'

There was a terrible silence. They all stared at me. Then Mum breathed, 'What?'

Dad shook his head as if he couldn't understand the words he had heard. Granda said, 'Aw, c'mon, Kelly,' as if I was kidding. He was the one I tried to speak to, though I was fighting tears, and the awful morning had sent the Robin Hood dream away into a childhood that now seemed left behind. How to start? 'I thought she was rich,' I said, and then Mum grabbed me by the arms and shook me so hard, I thought my neck was going to break. I had never, ever, known she could be so angry. 'You stupid, stupid girl.' It felt as if she was spitting at me. Her face was twisted and ugly with fury.

'Margaret, don't,' Dad said, and Mum pushed me away, letting go of my arms, but she came after me, still shouting in my face. 'As if you haven't had enough! You take it all for granted, don't you, never think how we scrimp and save to give you what you want. And now this, just when your father's struggling to start afresh and we haven't twopence to rub together, you lose him the best contract he's likely to get, you wreck his reputation, you drag his name in the dirt — what are people going to say, don't use Ferguson, that lot are thieves? You greedy, selfish girl!'

I was in floods of tears. 'It wasn't for me,' I tried to say.

'Then who was it for?'

There was no hope of explaining all that and I was so hurt, being accused of greed. 'I didn't know we—'

'Didn't know what?'

'That we were poor.'

'Ach, Kelly, they didny want to worry you,' Granda said, but Mum rounded on him and snapped, 'You keep out of this.'

Dad was quieter, but grim-faced. He said, 'Where's the money, Kelly?'

'I gave it away.'

'Gave it away?' Mum shrieked. 'Well, you can just go and get it right back again.'

'I can't.'

Dad said, 'Who did you give it to?'

'Lots of people. This morning. In Argyle Street.' The words came between great shaking sobs. Mum pushed a box of tissues at me and snapped, 'Blow your nose,' and I groped for one and got too many.

Then Granda said, 'Feed the poor. Was that it, Kelly?'

I nodded, and was overwhelmed by a fresh flood of tears. He hobbled over to me and put his arm round my shoulders, and I turned to him and buried my face in the comforting woolliness of his jersey.

'Oh, charming,' Mum said. 'Playing the Lady Bountiful, were you, with your stolen money?' And there was a lot more. I could not believe this was my careful mother who worried over me and never said anything hasty or ill-judged, pouring out these blistering, sarcastic words.

Oh, Mum, I said to myself in Miss Currie's English lesson, I wish — but even in the privacy of my own mind, I could not complete the words, 'I wish you loved me.' And I knew I was going to cry. All the dreadful silence of this last year, when no reference was made to what I had done, meant I was not forgiven. It was too bad to be talked about. I was too bad to be loved.

Ross said, 'Hey, Miss, Kelly's crying.'

Miss Currie said kindly, 'What is it, Kelly?' But I couldn't speak. Everyone was looking. Angie put her hand over mine, but I shook it off, and the movement somehow charged me with a mad electricity, and I was out of my desk and through the door and down the corridor, running past the big, bare windows, past an empty Coke can on the floor, through the double doors, down the stairs. Someone behind me. 'Kelly, wait!' Angie.

I stopped on the half-landing to let her catch up. 'What is it?' she said. 'What's the matter?'

'It's this horrible Project,' I wept. 'Raking it all up. I can't bear it.'

She looked stunned. 'But you were just writing a list, it wasn't anything personal, it could be anyone.'

'But it wasn't anyone, it was *me*!' I yelled. Poor Angie, it wasn't her fault, but suddenly I was raging. 'You're so blasted clever!' I screamed at her, 'You don't understand, you didn't listen, you didn't care. I'm sick of it.' I pelted off down the stone steps. 'And don't come after me!' I yelled over my shoulder, 'Just leave me alone!'

That last glimpse of her appalled face was still with me as I hurtled out of the building and across the tarmac yard and out of the gate. I ran away from the dreadfulness of everything, the school with its wire-mesh windows and graffiti, Ross and the other boys who sent me up because I didn't talk like them, Miss Currie with her patronizing smile and her kindly encouragement of any half-baked idea as if I was an idiot, Ian, who didn't write to me even though he'd promised. And Mum, oh, my mother, who had turned into a woman I could never please.

CHAPTER 10

I ran until my chest was aching. By that time, I had stopped crying, and my fury was ebbing away. I walked past a bottle shop with its steel-mesh shutters still in place over the windows, and looked away because it reminded me of school, where there were the same kind of grids and bars against the people who might break in at night and pinch the computers or burn the place down. Then there was an estate agent and a building society and a clothes shop called Nearly New, and a baker's. The shelves in its windows were stacked with bridies and pies and currant slices, and my mouth began to water. Quite unexpectedly, I was ravenously hungry.

It didn't happen often, in those days. I always felt a bit empty, because I hardly ate anything – but I liked it that way, because I saved the money instead. It was stupid, I can see that now, but at the time it was desperately important. That morning, though, I went into the shop and bought a ham-and-salad roll, and ate it walking along the pavement, with the sun shining in that

Glasgow sort of way, windy as well, with big clouds blowing across the sky.

I began to feel positively chirpy. It was great, being out of school, nobody knowing where I was. And the ham-and-salad roll tasted terrific. It didn't last long, though – that's the trouble with eating, it's over so quickly. But I had some chewing gum in my bum-bag, and that's pretty good, because it makes you feel as if you're eating even if you're not. It's very comforting. I don't know why teachers make such a fuss about it.

Anyway, the next problem was what to do for the rest of the day. Being out on your own is great, but you need to know where you're going or what you're doing, otherwise you get that lonely, aimless feeling.

I'd just passed a bus stop when a bus pulled up, and I looked back at it and saw it was a number 44, the same route Angie and I had taken when we went into Argyle Street that awful day. So I got on it. At least I knew where it was going, and central Glasgow was a better place to waste time in than here. I showed my bus pass and hoped the driver wouldn't make a fuss about it not being school time, but, as Granda would have said, he wisny bothered. So I went up and sat on the top deck, in a front seat.

The last thing I wanted to do was think about the Robin Hood affair, but my memory seemed to have taken on a life of its own. I tried really hard to concentrate on looking out of the window, but the scene in our kitchen kept coming back, with Mum raging and me weeping on Granda's shoulder.

Poor Granda. He did his best to stick up for me. 'Ye canny blame her,' he said to Mum. 'She's jist a wean, she's no experience of life.'

Mum said, 'I can blame her.' But Granda went on arguing. 'Some folk care about justice,' he said. It was a mistake, though, because it annoyed Mum more than ever. 'Justice!' she said. 'Fine sense of justice, dragging her family's name in the mud. Who's going to repay the money she stole, I'd like to know? Jim and me, that's who. And I blame you, too, filling her head with all your Communist rubbish.'

Dad told me to get my coat on. 'And if you've still got the credit card, you'd better bring it,' he added. 'We're going round to see Mrs Melrose.'

'Oh, Dad, no!' Although I'd cut the card up, knowing I would never use it again, I hadn't dared put it in the bin. Dad told me to hurry up. And Mum said, 'Wash your face.'

I think Granda must have managed to do a bit of explaining while I was in the bathroom, because Dad was quite nice to me, once we were in the van. He started talking about Robin Hood, saying how different things were now from the way they'd been in Robin's day. There were not so many people in the world then, he told me, so it was easier to know exactly who was rich and who was poor. Robin's task wasn't easy, but at least it was clear. Nowadays, we couldn't all know each other in the same way, so we had to use mechanized systems instead, and things were much more complicated. I knew that, of course. I mean, that's why Angie wants to go to university and get to understand it all. I don't want to understand it, I think it's boring. I suppose I'm only interested in what I can see and hear and feel, really, and whether other people feel the same as I do. You can't tell, can you, until you understand each other? And that's got nothing to do with systems. But I couldn't explain all that to Dad. I just sat there and listened, and nodded, and wished we weren't getting to Mrs Melrose's house so fast.

I saw her open the front door as Dad was locking the van. Maybe he'd phoned to tell her we were coming. 'You had better come in,' she said.

Dad made me go in front of him up the steps, and at the door he said, 'Mrs Melrose, Kelly has something to tell you.'

124

I had started to cry again, and couldn't speak, but Dad was not going to help me. 'Just say what you did,' he said.

I brought out the handful of bits of credit card I had been clutching in my pocket, and held them out to Mrs Melrose. I tipped them into her hand, and some of them clung to my sticky palm. She stared down at them, and for a completely weird moment I thought she was going to laugh. The corners of her mouth with the pink lipstick on it twitched. Then she said, 'Well, well.'

I managed to say, 'I'm sorry. I'm really sorry.'

She led the way into the sitting room. Her handbag was not on the seat of the armchair by the fire, but she saw me look at where it had been. Dad sat on an upright chair, but she pointed at a low chintzy one for me, and I perched on the edge of it with my knees sticking up. I tried to turn them sideways, but it was very uncomfortable. 'Now,' she said. 'Tell me exactly what happened.'

I hadn't been expecting that. I'd thought she'd simply be furious, like Mum. Having to go through every detail of it was awful, because I didn't want to think about it. If it hadn't been for the Novel-Writing Project, I wouldn't have been thinking about it a whole year later, on the top deck of a bus.

She wouldn't even let me stop after the business about the card, she wanted to know exactly who I'd given the money to, so I had to go through what I'd done in Glasgow that morning. I didn't say anything about the awful man at the Low Level station, though, because Dad would have been so frantic at the thought of something like that happening to me. As it was, he sat there with his face very red, staring at the floor and frowning. At the end of it, she turned to him and said, 'Mr Ferguson, do you believe this story?'

Dad said, yes, of course he did. I could see he was trying to find some excuse for me. 'I think she got a bit carried away with the idea of charity,' he said, and Mrs Melrose raised her eyebrows and said, 'She'll have to learn that it begins at home.'

Dad coughed and said, yes, quite, and then he got his cheque book out and fished in his pocket for a pen. 'I expect there will be bank charges on top of the hundred pounds,' he said. 'If you'll just let me know the total . . .'

Mrs Melrose did not answer the question directly. She turned to me and said, 'Kelly, when did you cut this card up?'

'Yesterday,' I told her, still snivelling. 'Straight away, after I'd — used it.'

'So you only had the one amount?'

'Yes.'

'I see. Then there's really nothing much gone,' she said to Dad. 'And in any case, I'm covered against all but the first fifty pounds, so there's no question of refunding any more than that.'

'Oh, yes there is,' Dad said. 'Kelly took a sum of money from you, Mrs Melrose, and that sum will be repaid. What your arrangements are has nothing to do with it.' And he wrote out the cheque and gave it to her.

I thought of what Mum had said about scrimping and saving, and burst into fresh tears. Mrs Melrose folded the cheque between her fingers and frowned down at it, ignoring me. 'This seems a little hard on you, Mr Ferguson,' she said. 'I hope you're going to dock Kelly's pocket money.'

'She won't get a bicycle for her birthday,' Dad said. 'That's for certain.'

I blurted out that I didn't want anything for my birthday — and it was true, but I wished we didn't have to talk about it as if it was Mrs Melrose's business. Surely birthdays weren't just about money, were they? The idea filled me with a new wave of misery, and the worst of it was, I knew Mrs Melrose would think I was crying about the bicycle. I could see she thought I was a spoilt brat. Playing the Lady Bountiful, like Mum had said.

Dad got up and said, 'Right, Kelly, come along.'

Mrs Melrose opened the front door for us. 'Mr Ferguson, will you give my apologies to your young helper?' she said. 'What was his name – Victor? I'll be pleased to see you both back at work on Monday, if you're willing to consider the contract reinstated. I'll phone the police, of course, and explain what's happened.'

'Thank you,' Dad said. 'I feel pretty bad about Vik myself – he's a good lad.'

'I'm sure he is,' said Mrs Melrose. But she had not quite finished. She turned to me as if she'd just thought of something, and asked, 'How did you work out the code, Kelly? Did someone help you?'

I shook my head and sniffed. 'I just – saw the legs,' I mumbled. 'The three stools. I didn't work it out. I'm no good at Maths.'

'Neither am I,' she said. And she smiled. I couldn't believe it. After all that had happened, she gave me this friendly smile.

It finished me off all over again, of course. I wept all the way home.

And that was supposed to be the end of it. My birthday

was more than a month later, and there was no bike, of course, but everyone tried to pretend it wasn't a punishment. I got a sweatshirt and some bathstuff from Mum and Dad, and Ian sent me a silly card and a record token. I wished I knew whether he'd been told what I'd done. I couldn't face writing to him about it, not then, it was much too difficult. Granda gave me a big box of chocolates, and hugged me, and said, 'There ye go, pal,' but somehow I couldn't enjoy them. It was ages before they got eaten, even though I left them in the kitchen for people to help themselves. I think Angie had most of them. I'd gone off eating by that time.

Yes, that's when I started the Thin Fund. It was partly because of Mrs Melrose saying Dad should dock my pocket money, but even if she hadn't, I was still desperate to repay the hundred pounds. I wanted to save it up, and give it back to Dad, all in one lump. I got absolutely fixed on trying not to spend anything. Every day, I kept as much as I could of the dinner money Mum gave me at breakfast time. Angie noticed, of course, and wanted to know if I was slimming. I said yes, I was too fat – and the thing was, I did feel too fat, as if it was disgraceful to be using up all that money just to stuff food into myself. I began to like the feeling of being hungry, and every evening I'd put the money I'd saved into the big plastic piggy-bank I'd had for years, ever since I was quite small. After a bit,

I made a rule that I wasn't to put pennies or twopences in it, only silver coins. And then I stepped it up to fifties. People in shops are all right about changing small coins into fifties, they think you want them for the meter.

When I got off the bus in Union Street on that truant day, I had twenty-seven pounds fifty in the piggy-bank. And eighteen pence in my bum-bag after buying the ham-and-salad roll.

Shops seem quite different when you know you're not going to buy anything. They're just places to look at, like people go into galleries to look at pictures, I suppose. Food was the same. Most of the time, I'd just look at it and think how pretty it was. Like a painting. You can enjoy it without wanting to have it inside you. Sometimes there would be this ravenous hunger, but a salad roll was usually enough to damp it down, and then I would feel that I had been good, not wasting money on my greed. I mean, saints are good, and I bet they don't eat. Did you ever see a fat saint? They're always dead skinny, with that wasted but lit-up-from-within look on their faces, gazing up to Heaven. But they know God won't send them a beefburger and chips. Saints feast on beautiful ideas. And I feasted on shop windows, like a butterfly going from flower to flower. You never saw a fat butterfly, either.

That morning, I walked across Argyle Street and through the arcade, past the jewellers' shops with their arrays of thin gold chains round pale velvet necks, and paused to look at the Body Shop, all dark green and stacked with scented treasures, then out into Buchanan Street and up the escalator into Prince's Square. I'd never been there before. I loved its balconies with wrought-iron railings in twisted knots, and its big opal light-globes and the glass lifts sliding up and down between gilded pillars. So much to look at, I felt quite light-headed. Mexican papier-mâché birds, clothes in peacock-coloured silks, sweet-smelling bucketfuls of flowers, painted costermonger carts selling brilliant perspex earrings like Angie wears. If I'd had pierced ears, I might have been seriously tempted. As it was, I went out to the street again, and prowled through the other kind of shops, loud with rock music, where the clothes were nearly all black, and there were shelves of boots with three-inch platform soles. The ceilings were black as well, with spotlights shining down so you couldn't see the girders and flexes. And there were holes in the carpet.

Looking fills you up, like eating does, and after a while I couldn't take any more. I walked up Queen Street, past the statue of a man on a horse who always has a traffic-cone on his head. Angie says if the Council take it off, someone climbs up and puts one on again the next night. This particular day, the horse was wearing a traffic-cone as well, and that was a laugh. I went on into George Square, and sat down on a bench beside a petunia bed, watching some men load crush-barriers on to a lorry. There'd been some sort of demonstration or concert, I supposed. They're always doing something in George Square. Not tanks and banners, though, not like Granda says it was in the old days, even if he does believe there's a new rebellion coming.

I couldn't imagine rebelling, not any more. I felt too light and detached, like an empty crisp bag blowing about. Rebels had to be strong and heavy and determined. I got up and walked on, past Queen Street Station and along the road with the plant shop in it, with all those boxes of green seedlings outside, and little bushes with the roots tied in canvas bags. I turned up towards the concert hall and round the corner where there's Angie's favourite shop, full of silk scarves and joss-sticks and silver jewellery, then on again. Walking,

walking. Sauchiehall Street, British Home Stores, Marks and Spencer, Boots, Miss Selfridge, carpets, lights, music, square pillars with mirrors on them. I caught sight of myself in one of them, not looking empty and saintly at all, just a rather ordinary skinnyish schoolgirl in a navy skirt and sweatshirt, with lank hair and an unhappy face. It was quite startling how unhappy I looked, because I thought I was feeling OK, just walking about on my own, looking at things.

There was a *Big Issue* girl outside, shouting 'Help the homeless, please, help the homeless,' and I wished for a moment that I had fifty pence to give her. But I knew I wouldn't have done, not with the Thin Fund needing all the cash I could find for it. I sat down on a seat in the pedestrianized bit where they've got these posh black litter-bins with gold letters on them, and watched the girl. In between shouting about *The Big Issue*, she'd toss her hair back over her shoulder. It was long, reddish hair, and it made her look so brave and determined, that toss of the head to stop the wind blowing her hair in her eyes.

It might be me, I thought, standing there with a satchel full of magazines, trying to make some money. Nobody got like that on purpose, it just happened by accident because they didn't get on with their parents or failed their exams or couldn't get jobs. I could imagine those things happening to me only too easily – I was halfway there already.

The sun had disappeared behind banks of solid grey cloud, and the wind blowing along Sauchie-hall Street suddenly felt much colder. I'd left my anorak at school, of course, never gave it a thought. I rubbed my chilled hands together, and blew on my fingers, and wanted to be in the warm kitchen at home with Granda, drinking tea. But he'd worry if I got home too early, because he thought education was really important. I got up again, and wandered through the glitzy brightness of the Sauchiehall Centre, down its escalator and out the other side. A clock on the wall said it was only ten to three. I took as long as I could about walking to the bus stop, but a bus arrived at once, the way they do when you're not in a hurry. I didn't bother going upstairs, just slumped into the seat behind the parcel shelf.

Looking back, I can see how important it was, sitting in that particular seat on that particular bus, but it wasn't anything I decided to do, it simply happened in that way. I suppose it was what Angie calls Meant.

For once, I wasn't thinking or remembering, I just sat there like a great lump of nothing much, feeling glad the bus was warm. We were about three stops from home, and we pulled up at the shopping centre near the estate agent's where Mum works, and there she was, coming out of a shop with a pint of milk in her hand. And she saw me. Through the glass of the bus window, our eyes met, and I saw her mouth open to ask the question, 'What are you—' But the doors of the bus hissed shut, and we moved off, leaving her on the pavement, though I could feel her stare burning through the back of my head.

CHAPTER 11

I was in such a panic, I very nearly stayed on the bus to the end of its route, wherever that was – anything to avoid going home. Mum would be so angry, I couldn't face her, I just couldn't. But I had to, there was no alternative. If I'd been a bit older, I could have joined that world of people who lived in the streets and slept on other people's sofas or in shop doorways, but I was still only thirteen. I'd get put in some institution if I tried to leave home. And, to be honest, the thought of it scared me sick – even more than Mum did. So I found myself getting off the bus outside our flat, and climbing slowly up the flights of stone steps.

Granda said, 'Hi, pet. You're early. Did the school burn down?'

'No,' I said. 'I wish it had.' I felt very shaky.

'You want a cuppa?' he asked.

'Please.' I didn't mind tea, because there was always plenty in the pot. Drinking it didn't rob the Thin Fund.

He hobbled about, doing his bit with the kettle

and the teapot, looking in the biscuit tin, unwrapping a packet of ginger nuts. Then he said, 'What's the matter, Kelly?'

I shrugged. Where to start? There was so much. 'I saw Mum,' I said, because that was the worst. 'Just now. I was on the bus.'

'And did she see you?'

'Yes.'

'But ye didny speak to her?'

'There was no time. The bus went. She was coming out of a shop.'

He poured out two mugs of tea, then sat down at the table. 'So what's the story? Were ye out of school all the day?'

'No!' I was very hurt by him thinking I could have planned it.

'What happened, then?'

'It was English. This Project.' And I told him all about it, words tumbling out, probably making no sense, but he was great, he just sat there and listened. I got as far as the scene when I'd come back from Argyle Street, that I'd remembered in Miss Currie's lesson, and felt as if I was going to cry all over again, but I fought it off. I was trying hard to be sensible, because Granda really wanted to understand.

'So ye left them to it,' he said, helping me out.

'Canny say I blame ye, pet.' He sipped his tea and I sipped mine. It was very hot, and my lips felt trembly, so I wasn't managing very well. 'See,' he said, 'ye musny get it wrong about yer Mum, Kelly. She thinks the world of ye.'

I shook my head. I couldn't believe that, he was just being nice. Just think of it as fiction, I told myself, like Angie said. It's not you, it's the girl in the story. But she wasn't much help, either. 'This girl Jez,' I said, 'that we're writing about – she's supposed to be the hero.'

'Fair enough,' Granda said.

'But she's not a hero! She can't be. I mean, like Mum said, letting the family down and . . .' Oh, damn, damn. My eyes were filling with tears.

Granda reached across the table and put his hand over mine. 'I tell ye one thing, Kelly,' he said, 'it's never wrong to care about other folk. See, when yer Granny died, that felt like the end o' the world to me. An' ye know the only thing that helped? It was folk carin'. Mrs Khan next door, an' yer mum an' dad, and you, Kelly, an' the folks up an' down the street. This lassie in your story – I'd say she was a hero, right enough. I tellt ye once before, that was a brave thing ye did. It's no' your fault ye picked a way that disny work any longer, not in the times we live in.

138

Anyone can make a mistake. Ye've no need to go on doing penance for it the rest o' yer life, Kelly. The slate's clean.'

I said miserably, 'I don't think it is.' And at that moment, the phone rang. I stared at Granda in dread. It would be Mum, I thought, wanting to know if I was home, wanting explanations.

'Will I answer that?' he asked.

I nodded dumbly, and he levered himself to his feet and hobbled across to it. He listened for a few moments after saying, 'Hello?' (he never says the number like you're supposed to) and then said, 'Aye, she's here. You want a word with her?' He held the phone out. 'It's Angie.'

Angie! And I had been so awful to her. 'Hi,' I said.

'Hi. Are you all right?'

'Yes, I'm OK. Angie, I'm really sorry—'

'No, it was my fault, I should have thought. Listen, I told Miss Currie you had a really bad headache and you'd gone home. I said you'd been trying to make it go away by willpower but it hadn't worked. Is that all right?'

'Yes, brilliant.' It always amazed me, the way Angie could make things seem so normal. 'Where are you? What time is it?'

'Nearly four. I'm in the phone box outside

school, and I'll have to go or I'll miss the bus. Will I come in and see you?'

'Yes, please. And I'm really—'

'Don't worry about it. Oh, and I've got your anorak. See you soon.'

'Great.'

'Cheers.'

''Bye.'

When I'd hung up, Granda said, 'Did ye bring the paper?'

I'd forgotten all about it – shows what a state I was in – so I went down and collected it, and when I got back we had another cup of tea, and he ranted a bit about the state of the railways and the National Health Service and the evils of privatization, and then Angie arrived, and we retreated to my room with yet more tea and some ginger nuts, and for once, I had one, and it was surprisingly nice. She was perfectly calm about me seeing Mum, of course. 'No big deal,' she said. 'Just tell her you had a headache. Miss Currie already thinks that was the reason, so you're OK.' Put like that, it sounded so simple. But even having a headache in our house wasn't simple. There'd be all sorts of questions about how long you'd had it, and how often, and worryings about allergies and eye-strain.

Angie was going on about the Project. 'I don't suppose you'll want to know,' she said, 'but I'd just got it all worked out when you threw your wobbler. I had Jez getting rid of all the money, only the fat guy she pinched it from sees her in the street, trying to give a fiver to a drunk, like you did, and he recognizes her. Then when she tells him what she's done with the money, he feels a bit ashamed of being so rich and greedy, so he doesn't call the police.'

'Lucky old Jez,' I said.

Angie shrugged and said, 'We can do something else. If you hate it that much, we can start again.'

It was nice of her, considering how much work she'd put into it. I looked out of the window at the roofs and the distant sports field and the grey clouds. 'It's not the story,' I said. 'That's OK, really. It's just me. Having to think about it all.'

Angie said, 'But it's over, Kelly. It's just stuff to use, same as the things you learn at school. Even if you don't like them, they come in handy. Or they might do.'

And then I knew what the trouble was. 'It isn't over,' I said. 'It's still sort of – hanging around.'

At that moment, I heard Mum's key in the door. I knew it was her, because Dad is much quicker about it, just the scrunch of the key going in, then the door open and him inside, banging it behind him, but Mum usually has messages to carry, and she's got her hands full, and pushes the door shut with her elbow after she's put her keys back in her bag. I heard her voice in the kitchen, talking to Granda, and him saying, 'Now, wait a wee minute, Margaret.'

Angie heard, too. She said, 'I'd better go. What are we going to do about this story, then? If we're going to scrap it, we'll need to dream up something else. Like, before tomorrow morning.'

I sagged at the thought of it. And I didn't much care any more, one way or the other. 'You go ahead,' I said. 'You thought of most of it, anyway. If I drop out, I'll find some excuse.'

'Are you sure you don't mind?'

'Absolutely sure,' I said. And it was true. She could do whatever she liked with Jazz and Jez — they were not me.

'OK,' she said. 'Thanks.' Then she glanced meaningfully towards the kitchen, where Mum and Granda were still talking, and said, 'Best of luck.'

When she had gone, I didn't move. Just sat there and waited. It was quite a long time before

Mum tapped at my door. I said, 'Come in.' She'd never waited to be asked before.

She closed the door carefully behind her and came over to the window seat and sat down. Then she said, 'Kelly, how often have you stayed away from school?'

'Only today,' I said. Thank heaven she wasn't raging.

'Why today?'

I couldn't lie. 'It was this Project.'

'So Granda said. Is that the thing this writer started?'

'Yes.'

'I can't imagine what she thought she was doing. And I gather you used – something we both know about – as your subject-matter.' Even now, she couldn't put a name to it. She was being very patient, but I was still afraid she might blow up at any moment. Like that other time.

'It wasn't my idea,' I said, coward that I am. 'Angie thought—'

'I'm not talking about Angie, I'm talking about you. I can't understand you, Kelly. Whatever made you do such a thing?'

I muttered some excuse about not being able to think of anything else, but Mum brushed that aside. 'Just look what you've done,' she said.

'Upset yourself, upset me, upset Granda—'

'Granda's not upset,' I said.

'Yes, he is. He worries about you. We all worry about you. I don't know what's happened to you in this last year, you're in a constant sulk. You won't smile, you won't eat – it's so hurtful, the way you refuse everything I cook for you, picking at it as if it was poison. I don't know why you're being so resentful, it's not *our* fault that you got yourself into such a muddle.'

I couldn't believe what she was saying – she'd got it all so wrong. 'Of *course* it's not your fault, it's *mine*!' I said. 'You never let me forget it!'

Mum gasped. 'How *can* you say that? We've leaned over backwards to leave all that behind and make a fresh start.'

'I know, but—'

'But what?'

She was getting angry. The words I wanted to say rang in my head, but I was too afraid of her to say them. You don't love me any more.

'You're so distant,' Mum said.

Distant! That did it. I leapt to my feet. 'It's you that's distant,' I shouted. 'I know you never forgave me, but I'll make it up, I've got – ' I rushed over to the wardrobe and hauled the piggy-bank out of the top shelf – 'twenty-seven pounds fifty.

There!' And I dumped the heavy thing in her lap, and burst into tears.

Mum cried, too. She sat there with the piggy-bank in her lap like some pink plastic baby, and wept. I'd never seen her cry before. 'Mum,' I said through my own tears, 'don't.' I sat down beside her and touched her hand, and I still wasn't sure she wouldn't snatch it away, but she turned to me and said, 'Oh, Kelly.' And in the next minute, we had our arms round each other, and the piggy-bank rolled off her lap on to the floor with a great cracking thud, and neither of us took any notice. It felt so lovely to be hugged.

We sat there, not saying anything, just hugging and still crying a bit, but I suppose we were both thinking the whole thing over and seeing how the other one had felt. It's so easy to get it wrong if you're just guessing, you need to be told. At last I fished in my pocket for a tissue, and Mum dried her eyes as well, but when she looked at the piggy-bank on the floor, she nearly started again. 'I didn't want the money,' she said. She sounded very tired. 'I never even thought of it.'

'I know.' It had been my idea, not hers. 'But you said we hadn't twopence to rub together. And I'd always thought poor people were some-one else, they couldn't be us.' It was gibberish, but it was so difficult to explain. 'And then when you said about Dad struggling to get work, I knew I'd got it all wrong, and it turned out I wasn't robbing the rich at all, I was robbing *you*. Don't you see?'

'I should never have said those things,' Mum said. 'I've worried about it so much since, losing my temper like that. It's a thing I hate doing, because I'll say anything.'

'But it was true!' I said. 'And I'd rather have known. If we were having a hard time, you should have told me.'

Mum thought about it, nodding. Then she said, 'But I didn't want to worry you. You were such a funny child, you see, with your imaginings and nightmares. Not like Ian, he was so solid.'

'But if you don't know what the truth is, you've *got* to imagine,' I said.

There was a long pause. Then Mum said, 'Do you remember once, when you were quite small, I took you to the film museum on the South Bank?'

I remembered all right. 'Oh, yes, it was great, you could ride on that camera-boom thing – there was a Wild West saloon with swing doors.' But wasn't there something else, something to do with that day? Perhaps not, I didn't remember much about being in London. Maybe I didn't want to.

Mum was frowning. 'It was very dark, though,' she said. 'And they were running clips of quite scary films – *Dracula* and I don't know what. I always wondered if you'd seen something there that frightened you, because it was that night you had your first nightmare and woke up screaming.'

Then I knew.

'It wasn't the museum,' I said.

'What was it, then?'

The bad dream was there again, the awful familiar closeness of the flames, the watching faces, the helplessness of limbs which would not move, a voice which screamed for help but could not make itself heard. Was *that* where they had come from? 'Going home, we went down steps, through an underpass – a sort of circular place, with no roof over it in the middle, only it was covered at the sides.'

'The Bullring,' Mum said, 'by Waterloo. Oh, heavens.'

'And there were these people, with houses made of cardboard, and little fires burning.' There had been a man in a sleeping bag, we had to walk round him, his bare shoulder stuck out, very white, and he had his hand over his face, as if he was sucking his thumb. And dogs. 'There were dogs.'

Mum said, 'I was so stupid to go through there. I'd forgotten about it being Cardboard City – I was just thinking of it as the quickest way through to the station, without crossing the road.'

The smell had been terrible. And the people watched us as we walked through. They didn't move or meet our eyes, just watched, as if we were traffic, not people like themselves. It seemed different in the dream, much bigger, like some open field all covered with cardboard shacks . . . No, I hadn't known they were cardboard in the dream, they just seemed like walls, but the fires were burning on both sides of us, and we were a long way from anywhere, and Mum's dress caught fire, and I screamed for help, but my arms and legs wouldn't work, and the people just watched and made no movement, and my screaming was silent, they couldn't hear it.

'Kelly, was that it – those people, were they what frightened you?'

'They wouldn't help,' I said. 'Your clothes caught fire, everything was on fire, the dogs—' yes, I had forgotten about the poor dogs. 'But the people just watched. There was no *reason* why they should help us, I couldn't make them care.'

Mum stared at me, puzzling over what I had said. ' "I couldn't make them care," she said, repeating my words. 'I wonder if that was it. Your Robin Hood thing. If you helped them, perhaps you felt it would make them care. And then they would help you.'

'But that's awful!' The idea horrified me. 'It would mean I was just being selfish, not thinking of them at all!'

Mum considered it, then said fairly, 'No. If you didn't *know* you wanted anything, you can't have been selfish.'

I hardly listened. The people in the greenwood, with the sunshine filtering down through the trees, looked up at me with trust, and I could trust them, we were together. Was it nothing but a dream, then, the caring and the togetherness? I said, 'You can't make people care by giving them money.' I saw again the man who had scuttled off like a crab, clutching his fiver in case I had made a mistake, and the girl with the baby who had disappeared into the crowd while a woman told me how stupid I was to have given her money. But the boy with a dog had argued about taking it, and two men had refused – and there had been so many that I couldn't approach at all, because I thought they might be offended. Maybe money and caring weren't the same thing. But Angie would say that one was no good without the other. She was so practical.

Mum had picked up the piggy-bank from the floor. It was cracked right along its side. 'How on earth did you save all this?' she said, feeling the weight of the thing.

I blushed. 'Just – what was left from my dinner money,' I told her, not wanting to.

'Oh, *Kelly*.' I thought she was going to cry all over again. 'There was me, worried to death about you not eating, and you were stinting yourself for – for this. It's—' She ran out of words, and shook her head.

'I know. I'm really sorry.' And yet, I would miss the Thin Fund, in a way. You can get hooked on giving things up. It makes you feel good. Maybe I'd give up chewing gum instead, I thought. Mr McInch would be pleased. No, that was stupid. Mr McInch wouldn't even notice.

Mum set the cracked piggy-bank on its feet on the windowsill and said, 'Anyway, you needn't think I'm taking that money, because I'm not.'

I heard Dad come in. Now he'd hear all about it from Granda. Mum said, 'I'd better go and put the spuds on.' And I said, 'I'll come and help you.'

Well, that was it, more or less. Dad had doubts about the piggy-bank money. 'Tell you what, Kelly,' he said, 'you chip in, and we can get you a bike for your birthday this year, all of us together. Better than little bits of things. What do you think?' He was so unfussed and matter-of-fact, I couldn't say no. And it's been great, having a bike, you feel so independent. Mum always makes me wear a helmet, though.

That night, we had a long discussion about the Project over our beefburgers and beans and spuds. Mum didn't say as much as the others, but then, she never does. She said she didn't mind about *The Sherwood Hero*, though. 'In a way, I suppose it's cleared the air. And if you're sure you won't be recognized.'

Granda said, 'That's up to you, Kelly. If anyone suggests it might be based on personal experience, just look them in the eye and say, "What, me? Ye must be joking." ' He got quite interested in writing the story, and Angie and I had to restrain him. He was all for having Jazz and Jez start up a Union of Benevolent Burglars, to put the thing on a proper political basis.

As it turned out, our story didn't win, anyway.

Miss Currie said it got good marks for style, but the judges thought the subject-matter was unlikely. And we'd put in a whole bit about Jez getting put on probation, and checked out the details with Mike McKechnie, who knew all about it because his big brother had been done for pinching cigarettes. Makes you sick. Ross Craig and Jimmy Kelso, of all people, won it with their story cribbed out of *Miami Vice*. Angie was furious. Miss Currie was very nice about it, but she said nobody would give money away these days, would they? And gave us her kind smile. Well, what can you say?

Ian and Susan came up for Christmas, and we had a great time. Susan's really nice, actually – I can see why Ian likes her. And he and I talked about what had happened. 'It was a terrific idea,' he said. 'Robin Hood Rides Again. A real cracker. Trouble was, the supporting cast didn't know their parts.' We write to each other a lot now. I'm better at English than I used to be, so it's almost like talking to him. Sometimes he phones, but it's dead expensive, long distance, and letters are nicer in a way, because you can keep them.

Mum and I get on OK these days, and she doesn't fuss so much, even though I'm going out with Peter Carrick. But then, I'm getting quite good marks at school, and I painted the scenery for the end-of-term production of *Grease*, so there's nothing much for her to grumble about. Dad's fitted kitchens business is going well. Mrs Melrose let him take photographs of the finished job he and Vik did in her house, and that was a help, because it looked really good. Vik works with him all the time now, because he's finished his college course.

And Granda's enrolled himself with the Open University! He records TV programmes that come on at five in the morning, and bores us all stiff, reading out his assignments. Dad sends him up rotten, but he doesn't care. He's going to Summer School next year, a whole fortnight at St Andrew's, sticks and all. He'll give them a terrible time.

It was the Project, in a way, that started him off. He said I ought to write it all down like it *really* happened, never mind turning it into fiction, it was a good story on its own. So I did, as you'll know if you've just read it. He helped me with the spelling and suggested better ways to put things, and we argued about it a lot. But he got so interested, he started boasting to them in the library about it, and they gave him a leaflet about the Open University. He began with the English foundation course, but he says he's going to do Politics and Economics after that. Well, he would, wouldn't he?

Mum and Dad don't seem to mind the idea of this story getting published. I think they're so proud of me for writing it, my shady past doesn't matter any more. They probably imagine I'm going to be a famous writer like Willa Pargett, but I'm not – I want to go to art school.

Angie says, when she's Prime Minister, I can be her Chancellor of the Exchequer. You can't ask for a better friend than that.

And I got my ears pierced last week.